FIONN

STARLIGHT MERMEN

STARLIGHT ALIEN MAIL ORDER BRIDES
BOOK 7

SKYE MACKINNON

Peryton Press

To the finman in my life.

You swept me off my feet and taught me how to swim again.

Together, we shall weather all storms and surf the waves.

GLOSSARY

Eynhallow – a city on Finfolkaheem

Finfolkaheem – planet of the finfolk

Intergalactic Authority (IA) – space police

Intergalactic University (IGU) – the best and biggest university in the galaxy

Mooncrossing – a year on Finfolkaheem

Roussay – a town on Finfolkaheem

Span – a week on Finfolkaheem

Sunpass – a day on Finfolkaheem

PROLOGUE

Fionn

The planet's eyes were set on me and all I wanted to do was swim away as fast as I could. Hiding under a bushel of algae sounded better than ever. Internally, I was shaking, but I desperately hoped that the matriarchs wouldn't pick up on my weakness. My greenskin quivered ever so slightly, both from my own anxiety and the currents created by my clutch-brothers' suppressed trembling. At least I was not the only one who was terrified. And at least I was not alone. My brothers were with me.

The Matriarchs were taking their sweet time, discussing our fate amongst themselves. Lamina, the oldest and supposedly wisest, was scrolling through the test data on her tablet, her cyan lips moving as she voicelessly muttered to herself. I wished I knew what she was saying. Was there hope for me, for us, or was all lost already?

Time oozed along as slow as a mud tide. Couldn't they have discussed this before we were called before the Matriarchal Panel? Maybe it was for dramatic effect. They knew as well as I did that millions of finmen around the world were watching. During the six days of mate selection, barely anyone worked. Everyone was glued to their viewscreens, waiting to find out which young males would be the lucky ones that mooncrossing. Until today, I'd been one of them. It was a spectacle that brought us all together in a week of entertainment, excitement and lots of snacks, yet it also reminded us of our dire situation. The Matriarchal Panel hadn't been installed for entertainment purposes. It was all about survival, pure and simple.

Lamina cleared her throat. A tiny row of bubbles rose from her wrinkled greenskin as she repositioned herself in her throne-like chair.

"The Panel has come to a decision," she announced gravely. "Fionn Arken-Clutch of Eynhallow, are you ready to hear our judgement?"

I was not. Not ready. Not ever. Thirty mooncrossings of waiting had not prepared me for this moment. My greenskin was now visibly fluttering in the current. I no longer cared that they could see how nervous I was. The decision had been made. The time to try and convince them of my worthiness was over.

"Fionn," Rainse hissed from my left.

I realised the Matriarchs were still waiting for my response.

"I am ready," I said gravely. A bigger lie had never been told.

Lamina pressed her thumb to the tablet before looking straight at me. Her emerald eyes – almost the same shade as my own – bored into my soul, searching for weakness. I was torn open, broken shards scattered across the ocean floor, while Lamina pillaged my deepest secrets and desires. She didn't bother putting me back together.

"You are unworthy." Her voice echoed through the brightly lit hall as her words cut deep into me. "We have found you unworthy of the honour of being assigned a mate. Tomorrow, you will go back to your assigned profession and continue your life as an unmated male. Your test results will be sent to you later. We are very sorry."

No, she wasn't.

It wasn't unexpected. Nobody I knew had ever been assigned a mate. It just didn't happen to finfolk like me. Yet there had been that tiny bubble of hope, a quivering current at the back of my head that cold logic hadn't been able to soothe.

I was to be unmated for the rest of my life. No female, ever. Alone. Always alone. My clutch-brothers would remain the only family I'd ever have.

I wanted to cry. Shout. Tear down this hall and its panel of old females who thought themselves above me.

Somewhere beyond my grief and rage, my clutch-brothers were given the same verdict. No mates.

We were shooed out of the hall by impatient guards. I swam blindly, my eyes stinging with unshed tears. I would not let them see my hurt. Once I was home, in our cosy underwater cave, I would let my emotions free rein. For now, I had to keep it together a little longer.

"Fuck them." Cerban swam up to me, his face mirroring my outrage. "We never stood a chance."

I laughed, my voice harsh and alien. "Of course not. If it wasn't enshrined in law, we'd never even been given the opportunity to be in front of the Panel."

"What now?" Rainse asked. He sounded more depressed than I'd ever heard him.

I reached out and grasped his hand, then that of Cerban. "Home. Let's go home."

1

Two mooncrossings later

Fionn

The catfish bumped against my calf, purring happily, then wrapped its tail around my leg. Its black scales rubbed against my skin, tickling me. An explosion of tiny bubbles leapt from its toothy maw, indicating just how happy the beastie was. I tried to ignore it and stared stoically at the crowds swimming past me. None of them paid me any attention. As always.

Guarding the Great Archives had to be the most boring job on the planet. There was no reason anyone would want to rob them. In fact, nobody seemed to be even interested in visiting. In the three mooncrossings I'd worked here, I'd seen maybe a hundred finfolk enter the building. None of them had looked suspicious. Nothing ever was. The only vaguely interesting creature here was the catfish that joined me for most of my shifts. Giving it part of my midday meal was the main reason for that. Catfish were notoriously greedy.

I checked my commband. Barely a third of my shift had passed. I cursed the Matriarch who'd assigned me this job. When I'd trained to become a guard, this hadn't been what I'd envisioned. I'd hoped for glory, battle, excitement, not a life of boredom outside a library nobody ever visited. The only time anyone approached me was to ask for directions. Aside from that, I was ignored just like the building towering behind me. Some days, I felt like a statue, turned into stone by sheer boredom.

Something scratched against my hip. I caught the catfish by its neck, preventing it from sticking its head into my satchel. It meowed in protest.

"Stop it," I hissed without looking at the fish. As much as I hated this assignment, I still took it seriously. I wouldn't let this little beastie distract me from my duties.

It purred even louder at my touch, wriggling against my grip as if it enjoyed it. I bet I was behaving exactly the way it had intended. Little attention whore.

"I'm not going to pet you. You're not even supposed to be here."

It chirped with amusement, as if it understood my words. Catfish were incredibly intelligent, but they weren't classed as a sentient species. Most of the finfolk saw them as pests, but after the first few boring shifts, I'd grown fond of my purring companion. At least it appreciated my presence.

Even though it stopped trying to get to my food, it didn't leave my side. I refused to look at the fish, keeping my attention on the passing crowds instead, but I felt its presence. It was strangely comforting to share my shift with someone else, even if it was just a catfish.

A noise crackled in my ear before Commander Myke's voice made me swim straighter.

"Fionn, we've received a report of a disturbance inside the Archives, somewhere on the second level, right wing. You are tasked to investigate. You hereby have permission to leave your post."

It took a moment for me to register what I'd just been told. This was new. I'd never even been inside the Archives and now I was supposed to investigate them?

"Yes, sir," I said, keeping my voice calm. I didn't want to sound too excited. "I'll report as soon as I figure out what's going on."

Who had reported a disturbance? I'd not heard or seen anything out of the ordinary. Nobody had even glanced at the Archives since I'd started my shift. It was probably a false alarm, yet I couldn't help but feel my greenskin tighten at the anticipation of proper guard action. Maybe those two mooncrossings spent training to be a warrior had been worth it after all.

For the first time since starting this posting, I swam to the huge double doors leading into the Archives, each at least four times as tall as me. They appeared to be open, but it was just an illusion. The left side of the doorway shimmered silver, a telltale sign of an airroom. Some materials could not be stored in saltwater, so half the Archives contained oxygenated air. I turned right, staying in water. A shiver crept over my skin when I swam through the doorway, followed by a beep as the security scanner approved my passage. Nobody should be able to enter without permission; one of the many reasons why the Archives didn't need to be guarded by more than one person. There was another entrance, at the back, but it was permanently locked and hadn't been used in many mooncrossings.

The entrance hall lay abandoned. A few barnacles had started to grow on the marble walls. This building clearly wasn't cleaned very often. For a moment, I debated whether I should report it, but then decided it wasn't part of my responsibilities. Surely the people in charge of the Archives knew about the barnacles. I'd been told there was a cleaner who occasionally came at night, when other people were guarding the building.

Something touched my right foot. Acting on pure instinct, I pulled my weapon from my belt and swirled around, causing a stream of air bubbles to surround me. A happy purr made me lower my weapon. The catfish had followed me.

I groaned in exasperation.

"How did you get in here?" I asked it, not expecting an answer. The barrier must have been programmed to detect only finfolk, not fish. That would explain some of the droppings floating in the stale water. I just hoped the disturbance wasn't caused by some random sea creatures that had made the Archives their home. That would be one heck of an anti-climax.

I kept my weapon in hand as I swam up through the vertical tunnel connecting the floors. There were five floors in total, each dedicated to a different period of finfolk heritage. If I remembered correctly, the second floor held items from our more recent past, maybe a few hundred mooncrossings. Most of the contents had been digitised long ago, 3D-scanned and catalogued, making this building almost obsolete. Only the most passionate researchers made the time to study artifacts in person rather than look at them in VR.

It was gloomy up here. Some of the glowshrooms had died off, leaving patches of the wall in darkness, but there was enough light left to find my way around.

The silence in the Archive made me want to talk to myself just to hear some sort of sound. The lack of any current at all was almost as disturbing. Even on the calmest day, you'd always feel some movement in the water, whether out in the ocean or in an underwater building. In here, the catfish and me were the first to disturb the brackish water - well, us and the intruder, if they existed. I gripped my sonic gun a little tighter at that thought.

After three mooncrossings of imagining what the Archives were like, I couldn't wait to be back outside. At least the glowshrooms were filtering the water, adding oxygen and removing toxins, even though it tasted old and musty.

I swam right, entering the wing where the disturbance had been reported. Should I call out?

No, if there really was someone who had broken into the Archives, they might not come quietly if I asked them to. But who would even break in here when you could simply make an appointment to access the building at your convenience? I'd never tried to do so myself, but it sounded easy enough. Maybe this was all a test by my superiors. I'd done the same job for three mooncrossings without rising in the ranks. Both my clutch-brothers had been promoted in that time. Could this be it? A way to prove my worth?

The catfish bumped against my hip, reminding me of his presence. I was thinking too much. Had to focus.

With the sonic gun heavy in my hands, I swam on. My greenskin wasn't picking up on any currents caused by a potential intruder, but several of the rooms to either side of the corridor were locked with heavy portals that wouldn't allow any water exchange. Those rooms had to hold the more exciting contents of the Archives. In my induction, they'd given us new recruits a general overview over what was housed in the building but hadn't gone into any detail. We were just grunts to guard the Archives, not intellectuals to study the record chips and artifacts.

In this wing, more than half of the glowshrooms sticking to walls and ceiling had died off. The gloomy light made it all look even more abandoned. I didn't have to be a scholar to realise the wasted potential.

Wait.

A sound.

I swirled around, pointing the gun to my right where I'd heard a single air bubble bump against a shelf. I didn't see anyone. Nothing out of the ordinary. Yet the bubble had sounded too big to have been created by the shrooms. Someone had been here.

Slowly, I swam towards the sound, along a row of empty shelves, until I reached a round portal set into a wall that had become entirely dark. Glowshroom skeletons still clung to the wall, but there was no life left in them.

An iris scanner next to the portal was active, a single blue beam of light waiting for me to get closer. It shouldn't open for me, I didn't have the proper authorisation, but curiosity got the better of me. I approached the portal until I was close enough to the scanner. With a shudder, the portal opened into an airlock. Curious. I hadn't realised rooms in this part of the Archives held air.

For a moment, I wondered whether I should check in with my boss. But no. He'd tell me not to proceed. Whatever was behind this door was secret. The scanner had to be malfunctioning for it to let me in.

"Don't follow me," I told the catfish. "You won't be able to breathe in there."

It stared at me as if considering my words, then started to playfully bump against some shelves.

I took a deep gulp of stale water and prepared for whatever awaited me on the other side, then swam into the airlock. A contact plate on the floor was glimmering in a gentle pink. I lowered myself onto it. A strange fanfare made me look up in confusion. Not a sound I'd expected. This system had to be old, really old.

My greenskin felt the pull of the water before I could see the water levels sink. It started slowly, barely noticeable, before the current increased, drawing the water from the airlock. The process took a lot longer than it would have in a modern building. By the time my head was in the air, my hair heavy with water, I was impatient. Whoever was on the other side of the airlock would have heard it activating. They'd know they'd soon have company and had ample time to get rid of any incriminating evidence. Breaking into the Archives was a crime in itself, but theft or destruction of public property would carry a higher sentence.

Finally, the last puddle of water disappeared into the porous floor. I automatically arranged my greenskin over my crotch. Most finfolk didn't care much about that, but my clutch-mother had always instilled a healthy amount of modesty into all her charges. I shook the sonic gun to dry it. The sonic pulse wouldn't be as effective in air, but I was glad to have a weapon. For confidence. Just in case.

With another fanfare, the second portal opened, revealing a brightly lit room full of metal shelves covered in boxes, data chip tins and even a few old-fashioned kelp books. I took in my surroundings in a fraction of a second while searching for the intruder at the same time. At the end of the room, on the left side almost hidden from view by a shelf, lay an opened tin.

"Come out with your hands in the air!" I shouted with as much authority as I could muster. "I know you're here! There is no way out!"

A rustle from behind the shelf. My fingers tightened around the gun. I didn't know if I could truly shoot someone.

"Don't shoot!" a male called out. His shaky voice sounded vaguely familiar.

"Come out slowly!"

And he did. A young finman stepped into the light, staring at me with just as much surprise as had to reflect on my own face.

"Kelon?" I exclaimed. "What the fuck are you doing here?"

"Do I know you, guard?" he asked, a frown marring his exceptional beauty.

I wasn't surprised he didn't remember me. Kelon had always existed in a sphere of his own. One of the richest finmen in the city - not due to anything he'd done himself - he hadn't swum in the same circles as me in a long time.

"Fionn," I said, trying to keep the resentment from my voice. "We were in the same-"

"Clutch school! Yes! You have changed, Fionn."

I repressed a snarky response. So had he. Back then, he'd been a chubby finboy with few friends and even fewer achievements. He'd had little going for himself - until he got adopted by a Matriarch and his fortune had changed forever. I'd seen him on chat shows and in the latest gossip reels, pretending he'd always been one of the upper class. I knew better.

"What are you doing here?" I repeated rather than continuing with the small talk.

Kelon had the decency to look ashamed. "Searching for something. Not that it's any business of yours."

I laughed sharply. "I guard the Archives. It's *every* business of mine. What was so important that you had to break in? And why couldn't you just make an appointment with one of the archivists? Speaking of breaking in, how did you get in?"

He looked at me shrewdly as if to decide how much to tell me. Then, his brows shot up as he came to some sort of realisation.

"You're the same age as me. You were on the Panel!"

"What does that have to do with you?"

Kelon grinned. "You didn't get a mate. Neither did I."

I was aware of that. All of Finfolkaheem had gossiped about the Panel's decision. As the adopted son of a Matriarch, everyone had assumed he'd be given the opportunity to have a mate. Yet the Panel had rejected him. Rumour was that they'd had to show that they were impartial, no matter what family you came from. It had quieted the discontent for a bit, but not for long. Too many young males were rejected by the Panel every mooncrossing. Too many of us were desperate for a mate.

"I read something," Kelon said slowly. I was tempted to tease him about that - he'd hated reading as a finboy - but I kept quiet, letting him tell me his story. "There is a planet with females that are compatible with us. Yet the record I read didn't mention a name or coordinates. There has to be something about it in the Archives. Has to be."

"An entire planet full of females?"

"Well, that's what it said. But it was an old record. Things may have changed by now. Maybe they have the same issue we have. But they might not. Only one way to find out."

"Why-"

A crackle in my ear warned me before Commander Myke's voice rang out. "Do you have an update, guard?"

Kelon shot me a panicked look. "You want a mate too, don't you? I can help you. If we find the coordinates, I will send a ship there. You can come along."

I hesitated. Kelon had broken into the Archives, which meant he was now a criminal. I should hand him over to my superiors, maybe get a reward for doing so. Yet what he was saying... That ache deep inside my chest painfully flared to life. It had sat there ever since the Matriarchal Panel had spoken their judgement. A mate. I could have a mate. If I arrested Kelon, that possibility was lost forever. Even if I went searching for myself and found the coordinates of that planet, I had no means to get there. Kelon was rich, filthy rich. He could make the impossible possible.

"Can I trust you?" I asked hurriedly, aware my commander was waiting.

Kelon grabbed the greenskin beneath his left arm and bit on it hard. I squirmed a little, knowing just how sensitive the greenskin was in that place. "I vow that I will not betray your trust," the finman said solemnly, showing me his hand now stained with turquoise blood.

I grasped his hand. "A vow made cannot be broken without losing your honour."

He nodded. "Now tell the officer that you didn't find anyone. Then we can continue our search together."

I did so, my mouth tasting bitter as I spoke the lie.

"The sensors must have been malfunctioning," Commander Myke replied, clearly unperturbed and trusting my report. "Now return to your post outside the Archives."

"Yes, sir. Right away."

Kelon walked over to the portal, leaving a trail of tiny blood splatters on the floor. "There's nothing in this room. Let's continue our search outside."

I followed him through the airlock portal. In the water-filled corridor, the catfish was waiting impatiently.

"What's that thing doing here?" Kelon asked, pointing at the fish.

"It's been following me. It's harmless." I didn't see any reason to lie.

The catfish bumped against my hip and purred. I gave it a quick scratch on his scaled head, then turned to Kelon. "Where do we search next? I don't have much time before I have to be back at my post." The catfish nibbled on my greenskin. I pushed it away in annoyance. "Unless you can show us the records we're looking for, go away."

The fish cocked its head, purring louder than ever.

"It almost looks like it's listening," Kelon observed. I couldn't help but agree. The catfish's eyes shimmered with intelligence. I'd assumed for a while that it understood more than everyone assumed about catfish. Maybe it was worth a try.

I turned to it, feeling more than a little silly. "We are looking for records that mention a planet which harbours females that are compatible with us. I don't suppose - no, this is stupid. You can't understand me, and even if you did, why would you know anything about what's hidden in the Archives?" I shook my head. I'd embarrassed myself in front of Kelon.

The catfish swirled around in a circle as if it wanted to catch its own tail. Yeah, this was just a fish. I was an idiot.

Suddenly, it took off, swimming fast while continuing to purr. I exchanged a look with Kelon.

He shrugged. "I have no idea where to look next. We might as well follow it."

We swam along corridors, then up a tunnel to the third floor, before turning to the west wing. The catfish was waiting for us in front of a shelf holding record chips. Above it was a sign. *Animal Studies.*

I groaned. This was not what we needed.

I was already turning back when the catfish bumped against a record tin above me, pushing it off the shelf. It slowly sank down and I grabbed it before it could hit my shoulder. A faded label read *Fin and Ma'vel, A Story of Peritus.*

"What do you have there?" Kelon asked.

"Do you have a record scanner with you?"

He nodded and pulled a tablet with an attached scanner port from his satchel. Kelon had come prepared. I pulled the record chip from the tin and handed it to Kelon. When he pushed it into the scanner, I realised I was holding my breath. Beside me, the catfish was purring with satisfaction. If this ended up helping us, I'd feed it treats until the end of its days.

A document opened filled with tiny, yet beautiful writing interspersed with images. I increased the size of the first image, barely trusting my eyes. I blinked as if to dispel any illusion. This couldn't be.

A finman about my age grinned into the camera, holding a catfish with a stark resemblance to the one swimming at my hip. And next to him, an arm around his waist, was a female, gazing at him with pure love. Her skin was pale, lacking scales and greenskin, her features softer than that of a finwoman. She was an alien. She was hope.

"We have found it!" Kelon whispered. "We will have mates."

A mate. For me. I wanted to kiss the universe.

And that's when the alarm started ringing through the Archives.

2

Elise

My trainer's grave expression told me everything I'd feared.

"I won't be going to the Olympics," I said, each word a stab in my heart.

She nodded, sympathy reflecting in her eyes. "I am so sorry. It was a close call. But Jemima got better times than you three competitions in a row. They had to make a decision based on recent times, not past performance. Again, I'm so sorry, Ells. Maybe next time."

We both knew she was lying. There wouldn't be a next time. I'd reached, maybe passed my peak. I was too old to wait another four years. The Olympics were only a dream now.

I turned away from Caitlyn to hide the tears burning in my eyes. I'd expected this, but that didn't make it any easier.

The pool had emptied; all the other athletes were in the showers. The water was calling me. I dove in a perfect arch, the cool water welcoming me home. I stayed underwater until my lungs burned before resurfacing reluctantly. I didn't bother checking if Caitlyn was still around. I needed to think. And that meant I had to swim.

I lost track of the laps I did. Back and forth, never touching the pool's edge, one with the water, light and free. My arms and legs were heavy from exercising all day, but I had no intentions of going home. I'd only end up reflecting on all the mistakes that had led me to this moment. I didn't want to sulk. And cry. Yes, I'd definitely cry if I went home.

The pool attendant, grumpy as always, shooed me out of the water just before seven. As I stood in the shower, warming up my shaking muscles, I debated what to do now. I could go for a drink. Or ten. I'd earned letting off steam. There was no point in being at training tomorrow. I could sleep in for the first time in... I didn't even know. The last few months had been harder than any before. Until today, I'd hoped my injury hadn't held me back - but I'd been swimming with blinkers on. I was no longer as good as I had been before the accident. Now I had decisions to make that I had ignored for too long.

If I wasn't an athlete, what was left?

Swimming was my life. All I'd ever wanted to do.

And now it was over.

I slammed my hands against the tiled wall.

"Fuck!"

I was twenty-seven, with no degree, no skills, barely any friends. Well, friends that weren't part of the swimming world. Maybe my dad had been right when he'd told me not to put all my aces on my sport. At least he wasn't around to witness my fall.

A loud knock made me jump.

"Time to go!"

One day, I was going to shove that attendant into the pool. I got that he wanted to go home, but would it hurt to be nice?

Urgh. I didn't want to go to the pub. There would be people. I wanted to be alone. But not at home. So, what were my options? The cinema? Going there by myself was depressing. A long walk? I was exhausted and besides, it was likely still raining.

I kept debating my options while getting dressed and drying my spikey hair. Guess I could let it grow again.

It was more practical to keep it short when spending all day in the pool, but now...

Stop moping. Turn a bad thing into something positive.

My mum's voice inside my head made me smile morosely. She'd been one of the most positive people I'd ever met. She would have known what to do.

Something colourful beneath the bench made me bend down. A flyer, tattered and folded multiple times.

We are looking for women wanting to go on an adventure.

Referencing the Hobbit? I liked them already. I sat down and read the leaflet. It didn't give much information besides a promise of excitement, adventure and new experiences. That sounded exactly like what I needed.

See exotic places, explore alien cultures, meet new people - and maybe fall in love!

Tick, tick, tick. I'd travelled a lot for my sport, taken part in competitions all over the world, but I'd rarely ever travelled for enjoyment. I'd never had the time to take off more than one week. There was always training. And even when I had gone on holiday with my family, I'd had to spend hours in the gym every day and take care of what I ate rather than just enjoy the local cuisine.

Fuck. I hadn't realised just how much I had missed out on.

Exotic places. Escape from routine. If I was lucky, they had a trip leaving soon, before I gave in to the glum thoughts teetering at the edge of my mind already. Distraction was a great therapy.

I searched the leaflet for more information about pricing, but there was nothing, just a phone number and a QR code. That seemed a little suspicious, but I wasn't going to make up my mind just yet. I scanned the code with my phone and a flashy website popped up, full of pictures of gorgeous people in gorgeous places. One caught my eye, a couple walking in what looked like the Scottish Highlands, him wearing a kilt, her a beautiful white dress that could almost pass as a wedding gown. The way they held hands, their shoulders almost touching, made me jealous.

I'd never had time for a boyfriend. Swimming had always come first. I'd experimented with guys, most of them athletes like me, but it had never been anything serious. A heaviness settled deep in my stomach. I'd given up so much for my sport, my passion. But had it been worth it? I wasn't going to the Olympics. They might let me compete on a national level for a few more years, but then I'd be nudged to retire. What would I have then? Nothing but memories. And I'd be alone.

I forced myself to focus on the website and scrolled down, past the pretty pictures, until I found some more text. Most of it matched what I'd already read in the flyer, but a series of questions in bold, bright colours caught my eye.

> *Do you need a break from everyday life?*
> *Are you looking for new challenges and adventures?*
> *Could you imagine living in exotic places?*
> *Are you single?*
> *Do you want to go on a free, all-expenses-paid trip to a mystery location?*
> *Then fill in this form and we will be in touch!*

A free holiday? Surely that was too good to be true. It had to be a scam. They wanted my contact details to sell me something. That had to be it. I was a millennial; I'd grown up with the internet and social media. I knew what to look out for.

But still...

I scrolled down to the very end of the page to see if there was more information about the owners of the site.

Hot Tatties Dating Agency. Headquarters: Glasgow.

I blinked. I'd not expected this to be a dating agency's advert. Why would they organise free holidays? Were they that desperate for fresh meat?

My finger hovered over the button that would close the page. It had been just a dream, just a moment of hope that I might find new purpose in life. But all this leaflet had done was show me how I had sacrificed everything for my passion and was about to lose everything. I was at a crossroads. I could continue swimming until it no longer paid the bills, or I could make the decision to stop myself. Make plans for a life after. Take charge of my destiny.

I chuckled morosely. I wasn't a hobbit about to go on an adventure, leaving everything behind without a care in the world.

But why shouldn't I?

I took a deep breath and filled in the form. What did I have to lose?

3

Fionn

The Tidebound was sleek, fast and far too posh for the likes of us. I'd never been on a proper space cruiser before. The ship that had carried my clutch-brothers and me to the training grounds on the other side of the world all those mooncrossings ago had skimmed orbit for a moment, but it hadn't been built for long-distance travel. This one was an entirely different beast.

It was new and this would be its maiden voyage. The ship still smelled of paint and polish. The faint tang of metal and recycled air clung to every corridor. I didn't want to imagine how many credits Kelon had burned through to charter it. I'd known he was rich, but not this rich. It made me regret agreeing to work my passage. He could have afforded to hire a dozen more crew and let us travel as passengers. We'd gone to the same clutch school. Yet here he was, dressed to impressed and giving orders to the crew, while my brothers and me were busy carrying luggage into the cargo hold.

"How big is this thing?" Cerban whispered, as if he didn't want to draw attention from the other crew members mulling about the place.

I stacked my crate on another, flexed my shoulders. "I'm not sure. It's a long journey and Kelon is used to certain luxuries. He will have made sure he's got access to everything he wants. Plus, it's a hybrid ship, designed both for water-people and air-walkers. If what we found in the Archives is true, the females will not be used to living in water. They will need dry areas to be comfortable."

"I still don't know how we're supposed to be compatible with a species of air-walkers," Rainse muttered for the hundredth time. He'd been the most sceptical of my clutch-brothers, only agreeing to go on this trip because - in his words - he needed to keep an eye on us. He was the oldest of our clutch by less than a day, but he never let us forget that.

"You read the story. Finfolk lived on their planet for hundreds of mooncrossings until they were finally rescued. The mated couple in the Archives' record is only one example of many unions that happened during that time. Some even resulted in offspring."

We'd had that conversation before, the first time when I'd barged into our small home, shouting for my brothers in excitement, my heart still pumping with adrenaline. When the alarm had gone off in the Archives, I'd panicked. For a moment, I'd forgotten that I was a guard, not an intruder. But then training had kicked in and I'd calmly contacted Commander Myke, asking him to turn off the alarms, reassuring him that everything was under control. He'd believed me. Kelon had disappeared through a hidden side entrance with the promise that he'd be in touch soon.

And he'd kept his promise. It had been two spans since our first encounter and within that short timeframe, he'd chartered a ship, bought supplies and hired a crew. I didn't know what he'd told his family about his upcoming absence. Rainse, Cerban and I had applied for a week's holiday, our entire allowance this mooncrossing. Cerban's had been refused. He didn't care. If we found mates among the stars, we might never come back. A new life was waiting for us, far away, on a planet so very different from our own.

We'd done some research by digging through the Intergalactic University's database. After some dead ends, we'd identified the planet from the story as Peritus, home to a species called Peritans. It would be a long journey, much longer than a week. If we returned, we'd be without jobs. There were no laws against quitting your assigned vocation, but it was not something finfolk did. There weren't enough jobs. We might end up unemployed and homeless upon our return.

If we came back.

I loved Finfolkaheem with all my heart. The deep ocean valleys, the sparkling caves, the gentle currents, the kelp forests and long, sandy beaches, the waves that rose like mountains when storms hit. I loved surfing on the water's surface or swimming through narrow rock passages created by the volcanoes of old. But if I stayed, I'd be lonely for the rest of my life. No mate. No female. Not ever.

Other finmen my age had come to terms with that future. They focused on their jobs, on their passions, but not me, not my clutch-brothers. We couldn't give up on the hope of finding love. Even if it meant leaving our home and travelling across the galaxy.

"Fionn!"

Kelon's deep voice ripped me from my thoughts. The leader of our expedition strolled through the cargo hold like he owned it - which he did, in a way. He was dressed as if he was about to enter a boardroom, not go on a long journey through space. He smiled at me, but his eyes were cold.

"Have you settled into your cabin yet?" he asked.

"No, we've been busy loading crates." I tried not to let bitterness swing in my voice. Without Kelon, we'd never get to Peritus. And until the ship had launched, I didn't quite believe that he was really giving us the chance to come along. He didn't have to do it. He was powerful enough to simply silence me one way or another.

Kelon waved his hand dismissively. "You can continue with that later. Follow me. I'll show you." He lowered his voice, making sure only I could hear him. "I need to talk to you in private."

We had to share a cabin. It was tucked away at the far end of the crew corridor, barely big enough for three bunks and a storage locker. The air was thick with the sharp scent of fresh sealant and recycled oxygen, as if the room hadn't been aired since it had been built. One bunk was already pressed against the ceiling, leaving just enough space beneath it for the lower two. Whoever ended up on top would need to climb like a crab. Thin fluid cocoons lay on each bunk, looking decidedly too small for the three of us. We were guards. We were paid to be brawny.

We'd not been asked if we wanted one of the water-filled cabins instead of an air room. Some finfolk would have refused to sleep without the sweet taste and feel of water lulling them into the land of dreams, but for me, it was almost exciting. I'd never slept in an air room before. It was good practice for whatever awaited us on Peritus.

If we'd been assigned a water-filled cabin, I would have been tempted to take the catfish with me. It had visited our house every morning since that day in the Archives, as if to make sure we were proceeding with the plan. And we were. Hope was a powerful motivator. It was a pity to leave the catfish behind, but as soon as we were back, I would seek it out. If I found my mate on Peritus, I would let the fish into my home and feed it only the best fish for the rest of its life.

A single round viewport looked out into the dockyard, but the glass was clouded and smeared, giving us only a blur of light. No decorative panels, no privacy screens, not even a chair. Just a strip of neon-blue light humming faintly overhead, painting everything in a cold glow.

Kelon waited until the door had slid shut behind us, blocking out the noise of twenty-odd finfolk getting ready to leave. He swept his gaze over my clutch-brothers as if evaluating their valour.

"They can be trusted," I said firmly. "What did you want to talk about?"

He took another look at the door, then sighed deeply. "There may be a mutiny. This is my mater's ship, and half the crew are loyal to her. Once they realise that we are not on the way to a pleasure planet and are instead headed into the unknown, they might rebel. The captain is on my side, both through bribes and the promise of a female. He will cut communications with Finfolkaheem shortly after departure, so the Matriarchs will be none the wiser. But if crew members become upset that they will be travelling a whole lot longer than expected... I need to know you'll be on my side."

Rainse was about to say something, but I shot him a look. It was better if only one of us handled this situation. We'd all been in the same clutch-school, but Kelon had been closest to me – if an arrogant arse like him could be close to anyone.

"Why wouldn't we be?" I asked. "You are getting us to where we want to be. Of course, we shall be taking your side. Do you expect violence to erupt or just voices of discontent?"

"It is hard to know. That's why I want to keep our stay on Peritus as short as possible. Land, grab some females, test if we're compatible, grab some more females, leave."

I blinked, unsure if I'd heard him right. "Grab some females?" I echoed. "Is that your plan?"

Kelon ran a hand through his sleek hair. "Peritans are not very advanced, they're still inventing basic space travel. Their planet is under the protection of the Intergalactic Authority, which makes interacting with this species a crime. I did find a footnote about some kind of dating agency that has special permissions outside of the IA's regulations, but we don't have time for such nonsense. No, we will abduct the females we need and then leave as fast as possible. Understood?"

I clenched my teeth but nodded.

As soon as he'd left the cabin, my clutch-brothers let out a collective groan.

"What an idiot," Cerban growled. "How is a female supposed to fall in love with you if you kidnap her?"

I activated my holoband and the system interface appeared above my arm. "I'm going to search for this dating agency. I want a female with all my heart, but I will not go against what I believe is right."

Rainse put my hand on my shoulder and squeezed in encouragement. "Let me know what you find. Cerban and I will continue to work and cover for you."

"I will?" Cerban asked, his eyebrows raised, but then he grinned. "I will. For the greater good."

From: Fionn Arken-Clutch of Eynhallow

To: Hot Tatties (Director)

Subject: Inquiry into Matches with Peritan Females

Honoured Director of Hot Tatties,

Allow me to introduce myself. My name is Fionn Arken-Clutch of Eynhallow, of the finfolk people. We are an aquatic species who dwell on the world of Finfolkaheem, far away from your planet (coordinates attached). Though our bodies are made for water, we can also walk and breathe on land like yourselves.

I do not know how much is known of us beyond our own part of the galaxy. Once, long ago, a finfolk expedition ship was stranded on Peritus. For generations, our kin lived there among your people. Most returned when rescue came, taking along their Peritan mates. The names of one such couple — Ma'vel Skarra-Clutch of Wyre and Jonet Forsyth — survive in our Archives, recorded as true mates. Their story is proof that our peoples are not only compatible, but that love can exist between us.

I believe your agency, Hot Tatties, has special permissions from the Intergalactic Authority that allow lawful introductions to Peritan females. My clutch-brothers, Rainse and Cerban, and I humbly ask whether such introductions might be possible for us.

We are of good standing. We have no mates on Finfolkaheem — the imbalance of our world has left many finmen without hope of ever having mates. We do not wish to take unwilling females. We seek companions who might choose us freely, to share in life and family.

Please advise us if your agency can assist.

With respect,

Fionn Arken-Clutch of Eynhallow

From: Pam (Hot Tatties)

To: Fionn Arken-Clutch of Eynhallow

Subject: RE: Inquiry into Matches with Peritan Females

Dear Mr Arken-Clutch,

Well. That was not the sort of email I was expecting when I sat down with my morning tea. You'll forgive me if I had to read it twice. It's not every day that someone from an unfamiliar planet introduces himself quite so politely, and with coordinates attached no less.

I did a little digging after your message. The name Jonet Forsyth does appear in a few scattered records, sometimes spelled Janet or Jane, mostly in connection with a witch trial on the island of Westray in Orkney. According to the records, Jonet was burned at the stake, but I would like to believe that she found a new life with a finman. Interesting that your Archives mention her in particular. That certainly adds some weight to your claim. I have also looked up your planet in the databanks of the

Intergalactic University to learn more about your species.

Now, as for Hot Tatties. You're correct: we do have a narrow exemption from the Intergalactic Authority's regulations regarding Peritus. It allows us to arrange introductions between willing Peritan women and alien partners who have been properly vetted. Every match must be consensual. There is no "taking" involved — only choosing. Until now, we have exclusively worked with Albyans and Vikingar, but there is no rule that we should exclude other interested species.

The process begins with DNA testing. You and your clutch-brothers will need to provide samples for compatibility screening. Only if the system shows a positive match will introductions go ahead. It may sound clinical, but it saves a lot of heartbreak further down the line — and it's what gives our women the confidence to take this leap.

So, if you're serious, here's what I need from you:

- Full identity records

- Proof of standing in your society

- DNA samples from you and your clutch-brothers for compatibility testing

- A statement confirming you understand the women make the final choice

Once that's in place, I can begin the process of finding candidates. I won't sugar-coat it — our ladies can be particular. But if you're honest and respectful, you'll stand a fair chance.

Sincerely,

Pam

Director, Hot Tatties

THE TIDEBOUND

4

Elise

The dating agency had an office in an imposing Victorian building close to the centre of Glasgow. I'd had a meeting with my agent just an hour ago, gently preparing her for the end of my career. In the past two weeks, I'd come to terms with it and was now almost looking forward to a new chapter in my life. If this dating agency adventure didn't work out, I was planning to do some backpacking in Asia. Part of me was still mourning what could have been, but I pushed the feeling of grief and disappointment away whenever it threatened to rise.

Now I was about to find out if this adventure was going to happen or not. The agency had contacted me the day after I'd filled in the online form. A woman called Cleo had promised that this really was going to be a free holiday, no strings attached, and that I did not have to commit to anything. If I met a nice guy, so be it. If not, also fine. What I cared about was getting out of my familiar surroundings and routines and learning more about myself. About the person I was when I was not a top athlete.

Cleo and I had already discussed a whole lot of things over the phone, like what I was looking for in a partner, what my plans for the future where, and so on. This visit in person today just felt like a formality. I'd had to bring my passport so they could verify my identity, and Cleo had mentioned something about an optional DNA test but had been somewhat cagey about the details.

The agency's logo - a kilted cupid - was printed next to the doorbell. I took a deep breath and pressed the button. A light flashed under a small wireless camera installed next to the door. I waved at it. The door buzzed and I walked in, feeling both anxious and excited.

Cleo waited for me in a cosy office, most of which was taken up by a huge red sofa. She shook my hand before sinking back on a simple wooden chair, holding her very pregnant belly. Her ebony, glossy hair stood in sharp contrast to her almost porcelain skin.

"About ready to pop," she sighed in a gentle east coast accent. "Make yourself comfortable. I'm afraid that if I sit on that sofa, I won't be able to get up again."

The sofa was as comfortable as it looked. Two glasses of water stood on a fake marble table between us along with a bowl of chocolate biscuits. I resisted the temptation to take one, then I remembered that I no longer had to watch my diet and picked up two.

"We've already chatted on the phone but I wanted to welcome you to Hot Tatties anyway," Cleo said happily. "My boss, Pam, might pop in later, but otherwise this is completely private and nothing we discuss will leave this room. We value confidentiality and so do our clients."

I wasn't too fussed, so I simply nodded. Once I'd officially announced that I was no longer going to swim for Britain, there'd be nobody in the media or public interested in who I dated. Unless she meant the guys.

"Do you advertise for men the same way you do for women?" I asked. "With ads promising adventure and free holidays?"

Cleo smiled. "No. Most of our male clients come to us directly in search for partners. It is how we finance our work. We regularly get donations from happy clients who found their mat-, I mean, who found love through our agency."

For a moment, I felt the whole thing was a little seedy. Men paying to be matched with women without having to do the legwork themselves. But then, I was doing the same thing. I could have downloaded a dating app.

Instead, I was sitting on the world's most comfortable sofa.

"Does that mean most of your male clients are well off?"

Please give me a billionaire.

Cleo shook her head. "Some are, some aren't. Just yesterday, we added three new gentlemen to our database who are from abroad and whose currency is difficult to match up with our own. But that didn't matter. We vetted them and thought they were great candidates for some of our ladies. Anyway, I don't want to keep you for too long. I have two things to discuss with you today."

She pulled a small plastic vial from her pocket. "As I mentioned on the phone, we'd like to offer you a DNA test. Together with a university, we have developed a unique, patented way to find romantic matches. All you have to do is spit in the tube, we'll get certain markers in your DNA analysed and uploaded to the database, and our algorithm will do the rest." She suddenly stopped and chuckled. "Sorry, that sounded like an advert. But it really works. I've seen dozens of couples get together and describe it as being with their soulmate. It's more accurate than any other matching technology."

"What if you don't find anyone?"

"Then we will send you on that holiday to meet people we think have a high chemistry score based on your questionnaire and you might still find the person you want to spend the rest of your life with. Science is great, but sometimes intuition is just as good - and I've got a knack for matching people."

I shrugged. "Alright, I'll do it."

She handed me the test tube, and I spat in it, feeling slightly self-conscious. Cleo bagged it, then pointed at the desk behind us. "Would you be so kind to pass me that tablet. I feel like a right hippo at the moment."

I couldn't help but laugh as I grabbed the device. "Is it your first?"

"Third. And he's the biggest of them all. Anyway, we just got a new opportunity that I wanted to show you. You said you're flexible, right?"

"Yes. I haven't officially quit yet, but I think everyone knows it's coming."

"Good, because this trip starts tomorrow."

"Tomorrow?" I sucked in a sharp breath. I hadn't expected it to be *that* soon.

"I usually wouldn't even suggest it, especially as your DNA test hasn't been done yet, but I feel like this opportunity was made for you. I'm not allowed to give too much away, but let's just say that there will be a lot of water and swimming."

"Saltwater?" I asked in the hope for her to divulge a little more.

"Oh yes. You'll be surrounded by it."

Could it be a cruise? I'd hate that.

"Along with lots of other people?"

"No." Cleo grinned. "I can see what you're doing. I really can't tell you anything else. If you're up for it, all you have to do is pack a suitcase. We'll send someone to pick you up tomorrow morning and then you'll be gone for four weeks. You technically don't even have to bring your wallet. All expenses will be covered."

It was so very tempting. But I hadn't expected to leave that quickly. Could I really do this? Just pack my bags and disappear for a month? I'd have to call my trainer, my agent, my landlady, my friends...

But I wanted this. I needed an adventure.

I smiled at Cleo. "Do I need to sign something?"

I'd never been on a private plane before. It was just as glamorous as I'd imagined. I was offered champagne and lobster, a steward was at my beck and call, and the leather recliner was so comfy I fell asleep halfway through my in-flight movie. I felt like a rockstar.

They'd not told me where this flight was going, not even when I'd had my passport checked. The steward had said that he didn't know, but I found that unlikely. He must have been ordered not to tell me. But why? There was no going back now. I couldn't exactly jump out of the plane and swim home.

We'd been over water for most of the flight. I peered at the white-crested waves far below. We'd started our descent ten minutes ago, but we still hadn't reached land. It was all very mysterious. But soon, the mystery would have to be lifted. I couldn't enter a foreign country without knowing where I was.

"Cabin crew, prepare for landing."

The captain's smooth voice echoed through the plane. She could have just addressed the steward directly. It was just him and me in the main cabin. I'd expected more women to travel together with me, but again, the steward hadn't been able to tell me why an entire private plane had been chartered just for me. There were eight seats, but I was the only passenger. I ignored the niggling doubt at the edge of my mind that this was just too good to be true.

They'd want something in return.

This was costing them thousands upon thousands. The Hot Tatties office hadn't looked like they were making that much money. Not shabby or run-down, but ordinary, down-to-Earth. Not the sort of office where billionaires came to search for their arm candy.

Not that I was arm candy material. I was thin but more muscular and broad-shouldered than most men preferred. My boobs were small, my hair short, my cheeks covered in freckles. I could dress up if I had to, but I preferred loose, comfy clothes. And because I was so used to swimming every day, I rarely wore jewellery - not after losing one of my grandmother's earrings in the pool.

"Cabin crew, please take a seat."

A thin strip of sand appeared from nowhere, right beneath us. An island.

My heart beat against my ribs. Reality hit me. I was thousands of miles from home. I was about to go on the adventure of a lifetime. And I had no clue where I was.

The landing went smoothly. I tried to get glimpses of our location through the windows, but all I could see was a nondescript airport building in a sandy, flat place. Airport workers in bright orange uniforms swarmed around the plane as soon as we'd reached our final position, unloading my baggage before the gangway had even been attached.

The steward cleared his throat as he handed me a sealed envelope. Thick, luxurious paper.

"I was instructed to give you this upon landing. Someone from the agency was supposed to travel with you, but she had to cancel at the last minute. You should read it now, before you leave the plane."

I was about to pepper him with questions, but he'd already turned away, busying himself with tidying up the cabin.

I carefully opened the envelope. Ripping it open would have felt wrong. Inside was a letter, the top embossed with the Hot Tatties logo. Maybe I'd underestimated them.

Dear Elise,

Welcome to what we like to call the Island of Love. It has other names, but as it is a private island, allow us the indulgence of giving it a new name.

For the next four weeks, you will be sharing this island with four gentlemen, one of whom has been matched to you. Other women will arrive shortly. There will be various activities offered, both for ladies and for all guests together, including excursions to neighbouring islands. Please let the staff know if you have special requests or questions. They are here to cater for anything you might wish for.

Your first encounter with the gentlemen will be in a somewhat unusual manner. They have requested to stay hidden from view until you know each other better. There will be a screen between you and your accommodations are at opposite sides of the island to ensure you only mix once everyone is comfortable.

If you, after meeting the gentlemen in question, feel uncomfortable or do not wish to proceed with the dating aspect of this adventure, please let staff know. You will still be able to have a wonderful holiday in one of the most beautiful places on Earth.

Happy dating,
Cleo, Pam & the rest of the Hot Tatties

I read the letter twice. They were doing all this for four men? They had to be absolutely loaded. I doubted the agency was paying for all this themselves.

"Ready to disembark?" the steward asked politely.

I grabbed my handbag and took a deep breath to steady myself. I didn't feel ready. But there was no going back.

5

Fionn

Peritus smelled strange. The planet had looked beautiful from orbit, all blues and greens covered by white swirly clouds, but now that we'd landed, I wasn't sure I'd want to stay here for long. The air was dry, even though we were close to the ocean, and it smelled of sand and dirt and Peritans.

Walking on land took some getting used to. I'd visited islands on Finfolkaheem as a finboy, but it had been a long time since I'd stood beneath a sky so vast and empty. The alien sound of avian creatures calling out to each other was carried to me on the warm, salty breeze. Beneath the layer of animal song were the harsh voices of Peritans. Even with our translator implants engaged, they sounded so very different from finfolk speech. Our language was made to float on water, push through currents; a singsong that ebbed up and down like waves. These Peritans talked in a monotonous voice with little inflection or emotion.

But maybe that was just the males. The only female I'd spoken to was Pam, owner of the dating agency. After our initial messages, we'd set up a vidcall. We'd both been curious what the other looked like. Records on Peritans were sparse and outdated, while I wasn't sure if Pam even had access to information about us finfolk. I was still amazed that she'd somehow managed to cooperate with both the Intergalactic Authority and the IGU. Remarkable for a backwater species like Peritans.

"Remember, we only stay here for one of their sunpasses," Kelon said from behind me. "Then we take the females and leave."

He didn't agree with the plan my clutch-brothers and I had come up with. In a way, I could see why he wanted to make this visit to Peritus as short as possible. None of the crew had fully rebelled, but several were close. One, Lavus, was confined to his quarters after bragging to someone else how he'd find his own Peritan female and claim her for himself. He'd made it clear that he didn't care about the female's consent.

I'd been surprised when Kelon had locked him up, considering his own plan wasn't all that different, but maybe he didn't want anyone going rogue. He had to show himself as a strong leader who would punish those going against his orders.

Which was exactly what Cerban, Rainse and I intended.

The ship was parked at the very end of a long, flat island in the middle of the ocean. There was a Peritan settlement nearby along with a landing strip for their small, primitive airships. Pam had given us the coordinates. This island was private, where we wouldn't have to hide ourselves from prying eyes. Neither Kelon nor us had thought to buy camouflage technology to blend into the local population. Not that my clutch-brothers and I would have been able to afford such a thing.

"Did you hear me?" Kelon asked gruffly.

"Yes. I did." I didn't bother turning around. I was busy taking in the view. We'd landed only a short while ago but had monitored the situation from inside first to make sure this was not a trap. Now that we were standing outside the ship, on solid ground, the realisation that I was on an alien planet for the very first time hit me.

I'd grown up reading stories of explorers and space travellers, but they were always other species. Finfolk didn't travel beyond their own planet. It just wasn't done, except for a few traders and diplomats. Maybe it stemmed from that fateful trip to Peritus generations ago, when one of our ships had crashed here. Not being able to return home for so long must have been traumatic. I wouldn't have been surprised if the

Matriarchs of the time had disapproved of space travel afterwards.

Even more special that we were here now. And it wasn't long until we'd meet our first Peritan female. Pam had organised it all. It had been too short notice to find genetic matches in her database, but she'd promised that she'd fly in eligible females who she thought might be compatible, nonetheless. Females who liked the ocean as much as we did.

The sea called to me.

Footsteps behind me signalled my clutch-brothers' arrival.

"Is everyone finally ready?" Kelon asked, sounding bored. Did he not feel the enormity of this moment?

"Yes," Rainse growled. He found it hard to suppress his dislike for our benefactor.

Kelon turned to me. "Where are we meeting the female?"

"In the large building in the centre of their settlement. Pam says there will be a screen to hide us from view. She wants the females to get to know us first before they realise that we are not Peritans. Remember to use their language and vocabulary. Don't mention anything that might make them suspect we are not of their species. And-"

"Yes, yes. This is a waste of time. Once the other females arrive tomorrow, we will simply take them."

It was hard to hold back a sharp reprimand. Kelon was an idiot. No female would ever become his true mate if he took her by force. And what was the point of having a female that did not love you?

We made our way along the sandy path. A few Peritans, all male, shot us curious glances but didn't try to talk to us. They certainly didn't react as if it was the first time they saw an alien. They must have been briefed by Pam in advance. I tried not to stare too much. Their bodies were covered in fabric, even their feet. Some males had their chest bare but wore strange hats on their heads. Pam had suggested we don something she called 'trousers', but we didn't have any of those on board. I checked the fabricator but after seeing how these garments would imprison the greenskin on my legs, cutting it off from air supply, I'd abandoned that idea and stuck with my most formal loincloth.

The sun here seemed warmer than our own, painting the sand in shades of orange and gold. I had to admit that it looked pretty in this light. But I couldn't get over the smell.

At the entrance to the settlement, a male dressed in all black waited for us.

"Good evening, I am Paul Redfoot, the manager of the island. Can you understand me alright?"

"Yes, we can understand you," Kelon snapped. "Where are the females?"

Paul frowned at our companion's rudeness. I smiled at him to make up for it. Kelon didn't speak for all of us.

"Only one has arrived so far, the other two are still in transit."

"Two?" Kelon repeated. "There will be only three in total? That is not enough. That is not acceptable."

The manager shifted uncomfortably. "I only know what the agency told me. Maybe you can take it up with them? There must have been a mistake."

There had been no mistake. My arrangement with Pam was only for my clutch-brothers and me. I would not subject any female to Kelon's advances. But he didn't know that. If he did, we'd be out of here immediately, following his plan of kidnapping some random females.

"I will contact her after this meeting," I said as calmly as I could. "Kelon, I will deal with it. Shall we go in? This dry air is making my greenskin itch."

He shot me a sharp look but then nodded. We followed Paul into the building, where it was much cooler. In a large room with glass windows spanning two entire walls, a wooden screen had been placed in the centre.

On our side, a table had been set up for a meal. Bowls filled with exotic dishes were waiting for us. I inhaled deeply, trying to identify the ingredients. It was impossible. Nothing smelled familiar.

Strange utensils lay next to our plates. I'd have to look up the names for them later. In Finfolkaheem, meals were eaten on large seashells when in air-rooms, or sucked from bags when in the water. There was so much we'd have to get used to if we stayed here for longer than the one sunpass Kelon intended.

"Have a seat," Paul invited us. "I will bring in the female. Her name is Elise." He paused for a moment, then said quietly, "Please be kind to her."

He hurried away before any of us could respond.

Be kind to her?! How could we not be!

We were beggars on this planet, desperate for a female to treasure and cherish. On Finfolkaheem, females were precious. As the waters had grown warmer and warmer over generations, fewer and fewer of them had been born. They were special. No finman would mistreat a female.

I looked at Kelon.

Maybe I was wrong. Some might.

We heard them approach on the other side of the screen. The loud footsteps of Paul and lighter ones, following closely behind. That had to be her. A Peritan female. One chosen because she might be compatible with one of us. Not with Kelon. With my clutch only.

My heart beat faster. My greenskin tightened. My surroundings faded into existence as all my senses converged on her. The screen did not offer a single glimpse of her. But her scent hit me the instant she sat down.

Salt and wittleweed and nectar of pearls.

I gripped the edges of the table tightly.

I knew that scent. I had dreamed of it all my life, only for it to scatter when I rose from my bed, unreachable, at the edge of memory. But now I remembered.

There was no question in my mind.

She was mine.

6

Elise

The wooden screen was completely solid. I'd hoped for a lattice of sorts that would allow a peek, or a fabric screen that could suggest the outline of the person on the other side. Instead, all I had was polished wood, tall enough that even if I leaned back in my chair and craned my neck, I couldn't catch so much as a shadow.

I smoothed my hands over the tablecloth, pretending calm, though my heart was thudding like a drum. What was I doing here? Dinner with strangers whose faces I couldn't see, whose names I didn't even know yet. It felt halfway between a reality TV stunt and a very strange speed-dating event.

"Good evening," a male voice said, deeper than I

expected, with a strange rhythm to the words. "You must be Elise."

"Yes," I replied, relieved my voice didn't squeak. "And you are...?"

Before he could answer, another voice cut in, sharp and commanding. "I am Kelon. It is an honour for you to dine with us."

The confidence in his tone made me sit straighter. Whoever Kelon was, he clearly thought very highly of himself.

"An honour?" I repeated, letting a little humour slip into my voice. "Well, that depends on how good your table manners are."

There was a cough, possibly a laugh, from another male voice, quickly stifled. I bit back my own smile. Someone over there appreciated sarcasm, at least.

I didn't know what to say. Without seeing them, or their reactions, it was hard to hold a conversation. I took a few spoonfuls of soup instead. Fish soup with a fine note of lemongrass. Delicious.

If they were also enjoying the multitude of dishes arranged on the table, I couldn't hear any evidence of it.

This was awkward. To cross the silence, I asked, "Who else is there besides Kelon?"

"Rainse Arken-Clutch of Eynhallow," a melodious voice said from the left.

Someone else hissed something I couldn't understand.

"That is an unusual name, Rainse."

"It is to your ears," he chuckled. "Next to me are my brothers, Cerban and-"

"Fionn."

It was the man who'd cough-laughed. His voice was dark velvet on a warm summer's night. It had been just one word, just his name, but I already knew that I would listen to him read the phone book.

"Yes, yes," Kelon interjected. "Let me tell you more about myself..."

Kelon launched into conversation without pause. He spoke about wealth, influence, his family's holdings - things that felt like a cross between a job interview and a sales pitch. I made polite noises, but my gaze drifted to the solid screen, willing it to become transparent. I wanted to see the other men. Specifically, the one with the beautiful voice.

In a rare moment of silence, I was quick to ask another question in the hope that Kelon would shut up.

"Thanks, Kelon, that's a lot of information. But what do you like to do in your free time? Maybe the others could respond first."

Velvet-voice - no, Fionn - chuckled again. "I like the sea," he said before Kelon could start another monologue. "Not just to swim in it, but to feel it. The salt, the spray, the sound of waves against rock. It reminds me I am alive."

The words stopped me mid-bite. I swallowed, my throat suddenly dry. That wasn't the kind of answer you rehearsed. That was real.

"That," I said quietly, before I could overthink it, "I understand."

"I like to swim, too," Rainse muttered, but it was without the passion Fion had shown.

"All of us do." That was the third brother, Cerban. He laughed and the others joined him. I didn't quite get the joke. So they all liked to swim, so what.

"Tell us more about yourself," Fionn asked softly.

"I don't know where to start. Until yesterday, I would have told you that I swim for Britain. I'm on the national team. I was going to compete in the Olympics, but... Anyway. I don't. Not anymore."

"You no longer swim?" It was Fionn again, sounding sad for some reason.

"I... I don't know. I won't be competing. That was my life. Training every day, long hours in the pool and the gym. I'm not sure I remember the last time I went swimming for the joy of it. It's been about times and technique for so long..."

I stopped before I sounded melodramatic. A deep sadness washed over me. When had I lost finding pleasure in swimming? It used to be my refuge. Underwater, I could think. Peace and quiet. But then it became all about performance.

I suddenly wanted to run out of the building and into the sea, swim in the warm ocean, see what it was like. Reclaim the joy I'd lost. But I was in the middle of a strange first date with four men I couldn't even see. It was ridiculous.

Kelon's raspy voice cut through my thoughts. "As I was saying, I will be able to offer you whatever you want. A pet, your own private island, all the pearls in the ocean-"

He was back to his sales pitch. I had zero interest in the guy. It didn't matter how attractive he may be beyond the screen. I didn't like how self-obsessed and pompous he was. He didn't realise though. He kept talking without pause. I let it wash over me and focused on the food again. One dish in particular was so delicious that I made a mental note to ask the chef for the recipe. Some kind of white fish with spicy pineapple and pok choi. I could have eaten a second bowl of it, if I hadn't been so full already. And I hadn't even touched the four little desserts to my right.

"What's your favourite food?" I asked when Kelon stopped to have a drink.

I'd hoped one of the other men would reply, but Kelon was faster.

"Fish."

For his standards, that was an extremely short answer. I expected him to add something about gold leaf and pearl dust, just to emphasise how rich he was, but he refrained from elaborating.

"Fish," Rainse echoed. I could hear the smile in his voice.

Cerban chuckled. "Fish. If you hadn't already guessed it."

Fionn took a while to answer. "You wouldn't know the dish I'm thinking of, but one day, I hope to cook it for you."

Aww. If his cooking was as delicious as his velvety voice, I would devour it.

From the corner of my eye, I saw Paul, the island's manager, approach. This dinner was getting a little awkward. Maybe he'd remove the screen now so I could finally see the men opposite me. But he simply asked if we had everything we needed. Kelon asked for more wine. I hadn't even touched mine, sticking with fruit juice instead. I wanted a clear head for this.

Paul bent down and asked softly, "Are you okay, miss? If you want to end this meal, just let me know and I'll take you to your suite."

My suite. I hadn't even had the chance to unpack yet or look around the resort. Paul had collected me at the airstrip and driven me to this building in a little red golf-cart. I'd not seen any cars on the island, only a few motorbikes. Tomorrow, I would ask for a tour. And now, I really wanted to go for a swim.

"Actually, I think I'm done," I whispered back. "I'm quite tired from the long flight."

He smiled with understanding, then moved to the other side of the screen.

"If the gentlemen have finished their meal, the agency has prepared a film for you to watch. You will be able to meet Elise and the other ladies again tomorrow."

Kelon made a snorting sound. "I don't get to see her? I thought you'd remove the screen after we've eaten."

"No, the screen will stay in place until I am told otherwise by the agency. Please wait here while I escort Elise to her rooms. I will have a bottle of wine sent to your villa."

Kelon protested, but Paul ignored him without seeming impolite. I admired him for that. He must be used to dealing with difficult guests all the time.

I followed Paul out of the room, glancing back at the screen one last time in the hope that one of the guys might give me a glimpse of themselves. But no, they stayed sitting where they were. An enigma. I smiled to myself. I kind of liked the excitement and mystery of it all.

My suite was in a large building just opposite. I had a bedroom with a massive four-poster bed with dainty white curtains, a huge bathroom with a clawfoot bathtub big enough for two people, a bright sitting room with a small kitchenette area - I doubted I'd need that considering how good the food had been - and a veranda with an uninterrupted view of the ocean. A hammock stretched between two palm trees just beyond, inviting me to read and relax.

"It's beautiful," I told Paul. "I still can't quite believe I'm here."

He smiled politely. "We are very lucky to live and work here. Tomorrow, more women will arrive who will also stay in this building. We thought you might enjoy each other's company. There is an indoor pool, a library, a games room and a breakfast lounge. There are no set meal times so just turn up any time you're hungry. We also have room service, there's a button in every room."

"Thanks." I was a little overwhelmed. I'd never stayed in a place like this. The hotels my trainer had booked for competitions and training had always been basic. Swimming was a sport that didn't have the same funding as football or rugby, where the athletes were housed in much more luxurious accommodation. Not that I'd minded. It had given me the opportunity to travel and do what I was best at. Swimming.

As soon as Paul had left, I rummaged through my bags for my swimsuit. The sun hadn't quite set yet and the air was still warm. After sitting for hours on a plane, I needed to stretch my muscles. I grabbed a towel and headed straight for the beach.

7

Fionn

I couldn't stand to be in Kelon's presence for one more click. His behaviour had been despicable. I was glad the female - Elise, such a beautiful, melodic name - hadn't seen him. He'd alternated rude gestures with leering at the screen. I'd always assumed that other unmated males would know how to treat a female, but he had clearly learned nothing from his adoptive mother. He was self-obsessed, arrogant and selfish. My clutch-brothers and I had barely managed to get a word in.

How he'd lied. I'd been prepared to twist the truth a little to hide that we were not of the same species, but Kelon had taken it too far. I'd have to find a way to speak to her privately. Explain that she shouldn't believe anything he told her. Make sure she knew that he was a pompous arse who had never worked a day in his life, who didn't have a high regard for females, and whose wealth was not one earned, but inherited. He'd been the cutest finboy in the hatchery, that was the only reason he'd been adopted by the matriarch. It had nothing to do with his personality or valour. It could have been any of us. But I was sure that no matter how rich we became, my clutch-brothers would never treat a female this way.

He'd barely even asked her a question. It had all been about him. If it had been me in charge, I would have let her talk, encouraged her to share, listened to her beautiful voice that reminded me of the song of the starwhale. I would have made it clear that I was interested in what she had to say. That I wanted to get to know her. But any time I'd talked, Kelon had barged in while shooting me vengeful looks. He had conveniently forgotten that it was us who'd come up with the idea of contacting the dating agency, not him. He wouldn't be here without us.

Maybe I should have reported him back at the Archives and then found my own way to Peritus. But no, it would have been impossible. I didn't have the money, nor the connections. We were reliant on Kelon and I hated it.

"I need to clear my head," I said to my brothers as we walked back to the Tidebound. "I'll see you later."

I didn't wait for their response. I had to be alone. I had to think.

A small path meandered through low bushes and strange flowers until it got to the beach. I inhaled deeply, breathing in the salty ocean air. It was nothing like the sea breeze on Finfolkaheem, but it was still better than the recycled air on board the spaceship. I took off my loin cloth while walking. Sand squished beneath my webbed feet, first dry, then wet as I approached the water. My greenskin was tingling as it soaked up the humidity of the air. It had been too dry in that Peritan building.

When the first wave pooled around my feet, I sighed in relief. This was what I'd been craving. There'd been a pool on board the Tidebound, but it was always busy and the water had become stale after the first few sunpasses. I'd gone there several times a day to lubricate my skin, since most of our tasks had been in air-rooms, but I hadn't enjoyed the experience. I'd craved the sea.

And now I was here, about to swim in an alien ocean for the very first time. A smile curved my lips as I relaxed into the moment. The Peritan sun hung low above the horizon, painting the ocean in a spectacular display of colour. I walked a few more steps until the water reached my hips, then I let myself fall into the sea's embrace.

Cool water enveloped me. The salt tingled on my tongue as I took a deep breath, my gills filtering the strange-tasting water. It wasn't bad, just not what I was used to.

I swam further away from the shore endless sand gave way to kelp growing among large rocks. I took in everything, exploring leisurely while always listening for other animals in the water. There had been little information on Peritan creatures on land and even less about those living beneath the surface. I didn't want to be surprised by a predator large enough to harm me.

There were few left on Finfolkaheem; most had been hunted to extinction by my ancestors. But Peritans didn't live underwater. They might not even have explored their oceans fully.

A shoal of bright green fish swam past me. Little intelligence shimmered in their eyes and they did not seem interested in me. I went deeper, where the water was cold and dark, and tiny organisms danced in the water like stars. A large semi-translucent creature floated beneath me, its movements mirroring the currents perfectly. I swam alongside it for a while, watching and learning. It showed no reaction to my presence and I could not make out eyes or even a mouth among the pale jelly. Yet the creature was beautiful and I enjoyed its silent company.

After Kelon's endless speeches, the silence of the ocean was soothing. It wasn't completely quiet, no. Creatures called in the distance, short deep sounds that travelled far. Bubbles rose from the deep, bumping against my skin, making the smallest of noises. There was an alien beauty to it all, to the strange fish, the delicate jelly-creatures, the song of faraway travellers. I could have stayed here for hours. My gills had adapted to the alien water instantly and my greenskin was adjusting to the Peritan currents, reading them with increasing accuracy.

Maybe I'd sleep down here tonight. I had no desire to return to land. A pang of guilt hit me for leaving my clutch-brothers alone with Kelon, but they were grown finmen. They could handle him. And if they couldn't, they could join me in the sea.

I circled the island to familiarise myself with our surroundings. The land the Peritans had built on was just the top of a very large rock column that rose from the seabed, mottled with caves and crevasses. It was clearly volcanic in origin, if geology here was the same as back home. Small lights twinkled within one of the caves. I swam closer. The glow came from tiny bioluminescent blobs that looked not dissimilar to the giant jelly-creature from earlier. They clung to the walls and floated through the water, illuminating the space around them. I watched them for a small eternity. They were so simple, yet stunning all the same.

Some days, I thought life would be so much simpler as a sea creature like these. I bet they didn't have complicated rules and mating laws and rituals. They had it easy.

The current carried a new sound. I looked up, but the rocks blocked my view of the water's surface. With one last look at the glowing specks, I swam upwards with strong strokes, intrigued and curious. I would have recognised my clutch-brothers' movements; this was someone or something else.

When she came into view, I stilled. It was her. Elise. She was swimming at the surface, her body an elegant arrow drawing through the waves. Her arms and legs were bare, but a black fabric covered her torso and her hair. The sea made her skin seem greenish, almost like my own, but I knew that was impossible for a Peritan. Her movements were alien, nothing like the way finfolk swam, but they were smooth and strong. It seemed effective for someone without gills or greenskin.

Her head dipped occasionally, but not enough to give me a view of her face. Yet I was happy enough to simply watch her body. She kept her fast rhythm despite the waves, never faltering or stopping. Was she enjoying it?

Her words earlier had touched me. If I'd understood her correctly, she was an athlete who swam professionally. We had those in Finfolkaheem as well, although I had never been fast enough to be on the clutch-school team. But it had sounded like she'd lost all joy in swimming. I'd wanted to hug her when she'd said that, followed by carrying her to the beach and inviting her to swim together.

I hadn't expected to meet her now, here, just before darkness fell. But she was above me, unaware of my presence. I wanted to appear in front of her, talk to her, hear her beautiful voice again, finally see her face - but it would break the magic of the moment. She would see that I was not Peritan. I didn't want to imagine her reaction, but my brain tortured me with a selection of scenarios where she screamed in fear, turned away in disgust, cried at the sight of me. I crossed my arms in front of my chest. I couldn't surprise her like this. Cleo had been very clear that it was best if the females got to know us first.

And we were still waiting for the results of that genetic test. Maybe Elise belonged to someone else. Someone more eligible than me, someone who had a better job than guarding an Archive, more savings, a larger home - or maybe her fated mate was a Peritan. The agency had chosen Elise because they thought she might be a match - and now that I had seen her swim, I could see why - but that didn't mean she really was.

I hugged myself as I watched her swim back to the shore, away from me.

I stayed beneath the waves until darkness had crept over the land, mirroring my mood.

8

Elise

No other women joined me for breakfast. They must still have been on their way, travelling from far away. When I'd finished my pancakes, Paul appeared, looking bright and chipper.

"Good morning, did you sleep well?"

I nodded. "Like a baby. It's so quiet here at night, all I could hear was the sea."

"That's why there are no cars allowed on the island. We value peace and quiet here. Although I dare say that your schedule for today is looking rather busy."

He handed me a piece of paper and I studied it with slight trepidation. I'd hoped to go for a swim again this morning, followed by some time in the hammock with a good book. But the first item on the schedule made me look at Paul with excitement.

"Scuba diving? Are there any reefs around the island?"

"Yes, we have some beautiful corals. There will be an introductory lesson and there is the option of snorkelling instead-"

"I've been diving before," I interrupted, unable to contain my enthusiasm. It had been a long time. I'd had the chance to take some lessons during a training camp and had thoroughly enjoyed it.

"Excellent. Maelis, our activity organiser, will be pleased. She'll be able to take you to one of the deeper parts of the reef, maybe even one of the sea caves. She loves a challenge."

I grinned. "So do I."

I scanned the rest of the schedule. After diving was a short break followed by lunch with the other women. Then there was an icebreaker activity with no further explanation before a blind date with the guys. Dinner would also be taken together, once again separated by screens.

"Will we get to explore the island at some point?" I asked Paul.

"Yes, although there is not much to explore beyond the resort. A few pretty beaches, but that's it. One of my colleagues will be happy to give you a tour after dinner, if you wish."

"That would be nice."

Maelis could have been a supermodel. With looks like hers, I almost expected her to be a bit haughty, but she couldn't have been nicer. On the way to the beach, she told me her life story. Born in Barbados but brought up in England by her grandfather before she'd moved to Canada to study. Now she was living her dream on the island, giving snorkelling and diving lessons when there were visitors and simply enjoying life when there weren't. It sounded like staff on the island had a lot of free time. Maybe I could get a job here, should this dating adventure not work out. I could imagine living here full-time. I certainly wouldn't miss the Scottish rain.

She gave me a brief introduction to the equipment as a refresher before we got ready. I'd expected to just wear my swimsuit in these warm waters, but Maelis made me put on a thin wetsuit in case we encountered stinging jellyfish or fire corals. I'd never liked the feeling of swimming with a wetsuit. It was too tight, too restrictive. I missed feeling the water against my skin.

Last night, I had been tempted to swim naked, but I'd been wary of other people using the beach, maybe even the four mysterious men. I'd been completely alone though, so I might risk it tonight. There was nothing more freeing than being completely surrounded by water.

Maelis set a brisk pace, her flippers moving as one with her legs. She looked like a neoprene mermaid. I followed close behind, the feeling of the regulator in my mouth both familiar and strange. It took a few moments to get used to breathing through my mouth only, but soon I was able to focus fully on my surroundings.

We didn't need to swim far to reach the edge of the coral reef, maybe twenty metres beneath the surface. Golden corals were swarmed by tiny fish of all colours, hundreds and hundreds of them. Maelis signalled me to stop and pointed at a group of clown fish. If I'd been able to talk, I would have made a childish remark about searching for Dory. We watched the fish for a while as they dipped in and out of the corals, completely unbothered of our presence.

This place really was a feast for the eyes. So many colours, textures, sizes. I was itching to reach out and touch everything, but I knew better. Corals could die from human contact and there was no way I'd risk this underwater paradise.

Maelis motioned to dive deeper, away from the corals. While getting ready, she'd promised to show me a cave, which was her personal favourite. The water cooled down markedly as we swam down, leaving the colours of the reef behind us. It was darker here, almost gloomy. I half expected a shark or large fish to burst from the shadows. I wasn't afraid of sharks as such, but that didn't mean I wanted to encounter one here.

I preferred the bright chaos of the corals over this gloomy world where every shadow seemed to move. But at the same time, I was intrigued to see the cave. I'd never been this deep before. It felt like an entirely different ocean from the reef and the surface.

Suddenly, something rushed me from my left. Before I could react, it wrapped around me and ripped me away from Maelis. I was pressed against it face first. I couldn't see anything. It was a miracle my regulator's mouthpiece hadn't become dislodged. I was propelled against the current at a speed much faster than I could ever hope to achieve. I struggled against the iron grip, but my arms were pinned to my sides.

There was no way of knowing what had grabbed me.

I wanted to scream. But there was no one who could hear me.

The thing holding me swam fast, so much faster then I ever could have, even with fins. I stopped struggling for a moment. It was pointless. The grip around my chest was so tight that I could barely breathe. What even could this be? A giant octopus? But the body I was pressed against was hard and solid. It couldn't be a person. Nobody could swim this fast. Dolphins or whales didn't have flippers long enough to wrap around me like that. Sea monsters didn't exist. They didn't. Did they?

Until now, I'd kept my fear in check. Now it was threatening to break the dams and overwhelm me. If my regulator got dislodged, or if the hose connecting it to the oxygen tank got punctured, I had no chance of survival. We were too deep. I wouldn't be able to swim to the surface in time.

Forget fear. I was fucking terrified.

Would Maelis get help? We'd been in the water for about an hour. She'd make it back faster than that, but by the time she got to the resort, she'd have no way of knowing where I was. She'd had an emergency GPS attached to her wetsuit, but neither of us had expected to be separated. I was alone.

We rose slightly and it felt as if we were slowing down. Was my captor getting tired?

I struggled against the grip again, pouring all my strength into the fight. But no, fight was too strong a word. I could have just as well punched a rock. Nothing happened. No reaction whatsoever. It was as if it didn't even notice my struggles. I lost one of my fins. My only victory was being able to move my head slightly until I could see through the very edge of my mask.

Sunlight filtered through the ocean's surface. Tiny plankton drifted all around us, sparkling whenever the light hit them. A log floated high above, covered in algae and barnacles. I couldn't see the island, but my field of view was limited. I didn't want to lose hope that the island was right behind me, a refuge from whatever this beast had planned for me. We'd swam so fast that I doubted I'd be able to swim back by myself. I had stamina from decades of training, but swimming in the ocean was very different from swimming in a pool. If the current was going in the wrong direction, I could swim until my strength had drained away and I'd still not be any closer to safety.

We got slower and slower. The surface was only a few metres above us. Then the thing released me without warning. I flayed, trying to get my balance. My vision blurred for a moment as I adjusted to being still in the water, no longer dragged at breakneck speed.

The shape in front of me sharpened into something I recognised.

If I'd been on land, I would have gasped in shock.

It was a man. Almost.

He was larger than average, completely naked, and his skin was painted in shades of green, blending into the water around us. He'd attached seaweed to his arms, legs and hips as if to camouflage himself. He wore no regulator or diving mask, no oxygen tank, no flippers. But there was something between his toes, webbing, like a frog. It had to be some kind of advanced diving sock, even though I couldn't see where the sock ended. On his neck were indentations that reminded me of gills. But again, that was impossible. It had to be a trick of the light. His face was smooth, no beard, just like there was no body hair anywhere on him except for short black hair. His eyes glowed faintly in the water.

He floated in place without moving his limbs, only the seaweed shivered gently in the current.

I was even more scared now that I could see my captor. His eyes held no warmth, no mercy.

There was no way I could outswim him. He'd already proven that he was both faster and stronger than me.

How was he doing that? I was an almost-Olympic athlete, one of the fastest swimmers in the country. And how was he surviving underwater without a breathing apparatus?

Without warning, he swam towards the surface. His body barely moved, yet he arrived before I'd even started swimming upwards. With a few strong strokes I joined him. Breaking through the surface felt like tiny victory. I was no longer reliant on the oxygen tank. Up here, I could breathe.

I removed the mouthpiece and immediately swallowed salt water. I spat, then glared at the man.

"What the fuck? Why would you do that?"

His expression didn't change. If anything, it became more passive. "I am Kelon. And you are mine."

9

Fionn

Kelon didn't join us for breakfast. We had our morning meal on board the Tidebound, surrounded by other crew members. The atmosphere was loaded. Everyone had been disgruntled and angry ever since Kelon had announced that only him and the three of us were allowed to disembark. Even Captain Maggnus had to stay on board. Him and Kelon were chiselled from the same coral, haughty and arrogant, but if this situation continued for much longer, I could see the captain switch sides. Kelon had been worried about a mutiny from the very beginning. Maybe he had been right.

I didn't know what side I'd choose if it came to it. Kelon had shown his true colours in the past few sunpasses. He had no respect for females, no matter if finfolk or

Peritan. The only person in the universe that he cared about was himself. Maybe that's why he'd been chosen for adoption by the matriarch. He'd make a good politician.

Rainse pointed at a group of finmen huddled around a table on the other side of the galley. "They're plotting something."

I nodded. "We shouldn't stay here for much longer. I really want to follow the dating agency's plans, but it isn't safe. If they all decide to leave the ship, there's no way of stopping them. We're outnumbered. Kelon must know that."

"Have you seen him at all? He was very broody when we returned here last night."

"Isn't he always. I think I'll have a chat with Pam today. Maybe there's a way to accelerate the process. Add the other males' details to their database so they won't feel left out."

Rainse frowned. "I don't think some of them should have females. They're behaving like spoilt hatchlings."

"That's not our decision to make, though. They should have the same chance as us, don't you think?"

"I don't. Maybe there's a reason why our species is in decline. Maybe it's not just down to climate change, maybe we deserve it."

I put an arm around his shoulders. "Even if that were so, you deserve a female, my brother. And you will find the one for you. I feel it in my greenskin."

A twinkle appeared in his eye. "My greenskin felt a lot of things when I listened to Elise last night. If all Peritan females have that effect on me..."

Something cold and sour suddenly appeared in my chest. "She's not yours."

Rainse looked at me curiously. "Do you think she's yours?"

I knew it. Felt it. But how could I put that intense feeling into words? The urge to protect her no matter what, the desire to wrap myself around her, our bodies touching, becoming one, feeling her lips against mine, our souls linked until the end of time... Yes, she was mine. No doubt about it. I didn't need a DNA test to know that.

"If she is, you should act, brother," Rainse said softly. "Before Kelon does."

Whatever I was about to say was lost when Thallus, one of the more reliable crew members, came rushing into the galley.

"There's a Peritan outside with an urgent message!"

The room fell silent. Everyone seemed to be looking for Kelon. In his absence, I decided to take charge.

I stood, facing Thallus. "I will deal with it."

I ignored the murmurs of protest and hurried to the closest airlock. I knew Rainse would hold the fort until my return.

Paul stood outside along with a Peritan female dressed in a skintight black outfit that covered her entire body, even her head. She had a strange contraption on her back and a set of flippers in her hand.

"We have an emergency," Paul said breathlessly. "Everyone on my team is already starting the search, but I thought you might be able to help as well."

"What happened?" I asked. But I already knew. I felt it in my greenskin. She was in trouble.

"Elise, the lady you met last night, has gone missing. She was out diving with Maelis here, but..."

"She just disappeared," Maelis interjected. "One second she was right behind me, the next she was gone. It wasn't her first time diving so we went deeper than I usually go with clients. I wanted to show her what the locals call the dragon-egg-cave. I could see she was an experienced swimmer so I didn't babysit her too much, but maybe I should have..."

Her voice trailed off. Her eyes were lined with red.

Paul reached out and patted her back. "Don't worry, we will find her. As you said, she's a strong swimmer. She may have just got distracted by a pretty fish or coral and not seen where you went." He turned to me. "I've got everyone who owns a boat out searching for her. I've also asked for the helicopter on a neighbouring island to join the search, but it will take a while to get here. Can you use your... your spaceship to locate her?"

He clearly struggled with the concept of such advanced technology.

I wanted to run to the sea, dive deep and find her, but I forced myself to remain calm in front of these Peritans. "I will instruct them to scan the water for her. Can you tell me where exactly this cave is?"

I activated my holoband and opened a map of the area. The two Peritans gasped as it appeared in the air above my arm, but Maelis recovered quickly. She pointed at a spot south of the island, not far from where I'd been swimming last night. A coincidence or was the universe trying to tell me something?

"I will go there now," I promised. "I am fast. I will find her."

I sent a quick message to Rainse and Cerban with the coordinates and the request to make Captain Maggnus scan the area, then ran across the beach. The sand was still cool and wet from high tide but it was starting to warm. There wasn't a cloud in the sky. A beautiful day - except for that lingering fear in my chest.

And where the fuck was Kelon? I swore, if he returned and then complained that I'd taken charge and he hadn't been informed... I'd need both my clutch-brothers to restrain me.

The ocean welcomed me like an old friend. I swam as fast as I could, piercing through the waves, my long hair slapping against my back. My greenskin kept me on course, adjusting my swim direction ever so slightly when needed. I passed a large mammal which looked at me curiously from dark, intelligent eyes. I doubted my translator implant would work for Peritan animals, otherwise I could have asked it to join the search.

It didn't take long to reach the cave entrance where Elise had last been seen. Jelly creatures floated in the water, moving majestically on the current. If I'd not been here to search for a missing female, I would have stopped to admire the sight. But a sense of urgency filled me. I knew Elise was in trouble. She hadn't just got lost. I didn't know how I could be so sure, but I would have sworn anything on it. She needed help. Now I just had to find her.

I stilled my greenskin and listened to the sounds of the ocean. I closed my eyes, straining to hear anything out of the ordinary. I was glad I'd been for a swim last night to familiarise myself with this planet's ocean. I knew now what it should sound like. No matter how hard I focused, I couldn't sense anything that would give me reason to suspect it was Elise.

So much for that plan. I could wait until the Tidebound scanned the sea, but no. I had to do something.

The ache in my chest was growing deeper. For a moment, fear for Elise clouded my judgement and I simply swam, as if pulled by a thread attached right to my heart. Then I stopped. It was silly. I couldn't just swim in a random direction and hope for the best. I had to be strategic about it. But...

It felt right. Instinctively, I *knew* where to go. That pull told me.

I was a rational finman. I'd always preferred to think and strategize rather than rush into action. But Elise was in danger. Maybe it was time to throw caution in the wind and listen to my instincts.

So I swam.

I became one with the sea, taking advantage of its ripples and currents, moving faster than I ever had before. My muscles ached, my gills hurt from lack of oxygen, but I kept swimming, drawn by the invisible thread pulling at my chest. It was leading me to her. My female. My mate.

I heard them before I could see them through the hazy water. A familiar, cold voice that carried far.

I balled my hands into fists. What the fuck was Kelon doing out here? Had he stumbled across Elise by accident? Or was her disappearance his fault?

Either way, he shouldn't be alone with her. It wasn't safe. He'd made it very clear what he thought of females.

I grit my teeth and increased my pace even more until my muscles burned in protest. There they were, two shapes swimming close to each other. Kelon held steady in the waves, his greenskin stabilising him as it should, but Elise was being pushed around, struggling to stay afloat. He didn't reach out to help her. He simply watched.

I was going to kill him.

I dove deeper in order to catch him off guard. When I was right underneath them, I swam up fast, grabbed his ankles and pulled him down. He shrieked in surprise but it didn't take him long to recover. He kicked back with his right foot, narrowly missing my head, but I didn't let go.

"Let go!" he shouted, his sharp voice an ugly contrast to the beauty of the ocean.

"What did you do to her?" I yelled, still pulling him down further. "Did you hurt her?"

"I was just going to have some fun," he growled. "Let me go, Fionn! You're going to regret this."

"There's no way I'll let you go back to her. You've done enough damage already."

"Damage?" He laughed. "She's mine. I can do with her however I please."

I let go of his ankles, swam up a tiny bit and kicked him in the stomach. He cried out and bowed over.

"She is not yours!" I shouted. "She will never be yours!"

To my surprise, he laughed. "And you think you can have her? A lowly guard, penniless, unworthy, the scum of society? You will never have a female. Not here, not on Finfolkaheem, not anywhere."

I could no longer think. Fury ruled me. I put my hands around his throat and squeezed. A lowly guard? I'd done two mooncrossings of training. The same training soldiers did. I was a warrior. I was stronger than him.

He tried to speak, tried to defend himself. His fingers clawed at my face, ripping through skin. He kicked me, again and again. But I didn't let go.

He'd threatened my mate. I could not let him go.

If it hadn't been for my holoband vibrating urgently, I don't know how far I would have gone.

The vibrations were just enough to push through the haze of anger to make me see what was happening. Kelon had stopped fighting. He was still breathing, short struggling breaths, but he was out cold.

I let go of him, disgusted with both him and myself, before taking the call.

"We've got a lock on her," Rainse said without preamble. "And I see you and Kelon are close by. Want me to bring you all on board?"

"No." My voice was harsh and raspy. I didn't recognise myself. "Kelon will make his own way back. And I will take Elise, unless you see any injuries?"

"None that our scanners could find. Are you sure about this, Fionn?"

I set my jaw. "No. But I will do it anyway."

I let Kelon sink into the depths of the ocean. Finfolk couldn't drown. He'd swim back when he regained consciousness. It would give Elise and me a head start. What we would do once we reached the island... I didn't know. Kelon would be furious. Best case scenario, he'd leave my brothers and me on Peritus as castaways. I didn't want to think about what else he might do to us. Or to Elise.

I'd keep her safe. It was the one and only duty left in my life.

With one last look at Kelon's prone body, I swam upwards, towards Elise.

10

Elise

I was treading water, but the waves were growing higher and higher. My eyes stung with saltwater, my mouth was dry, my throat sore. I ached everywhere.

Kelon had ripped off my mask and regulator when I'd told him that I wasn't going to be his wife. It had been swept away.

But now he was gone and I was alone. I couldn't see the island. Nothing but churning waves under a cloudless, searing sky. I had no compass, no way of knowing where I was. Even if the sun wasn't right above me so I could use it as a guide, I didn't know in which direction Kelon had dragged me.

He hadn't said much. He hadn't explained how he'd swam so fast or why he had green paint smeared all over his body. All he'd kept repeating was that I belonged to him. He'd not listened to me.

I was going to have a long, deep talk to the dating agency for allowing someone like him to be part of the process. He wasn't safe to be around women. His views were more than just antiquated. He wanted a woman as his possession, not as his partner and companion. Fuck him.

I took a deep breath and let myself sink underneath the surface again to search for him again. Nothing. One second he'd been threatening to take me against my will, the next he was gone, pulled under by an unseen force. I almost hoped it was a shark. But no, that wasn't me. I never wished bad things on anyone. Not even Kelon.

But he had been gone for at least five minutes now. He wasn't wearing a breathing apparatus - but he had survived our swim earlier, and not just survived, he had set a new speed record underwater. I didn't know how he'd done it. I was desperate to know, but first I had to get back onto land.

I resurfaced, my eyes burning. I wished he hadn't taken away my mask. I surveyed the water around me once more, searching for a glimpse of land. No luck. But there was the log that I'd seen from underneath, bobbing on the waves. Adrenaline was starting to give way to exhaustion. I wouldn't be able to swim forever. I shot one last glance into the darkness beneath my feet and swam towards the log.

I almost didn't hear the voice among the sound of the waves.

"And where do you think you're going?"

I swirled around to find myself face to face with another man. I knew that velvety voice, although it was grave now, not as light as during dinner. Fionn.

"Yes, that's me."

I hadn't even realised I'd said his name aloud.

So this was what he looked like. Long dark hair that shimmered green, but that had to be a trick of the light. Everything about him was angular, chiselled, from the square jaw to the almost triangular eyebrows above dark green eyes. Just like Kelon's, his face had been painted shades of green and turquoise. Maybe it was a cultural thing? Or had they been taking part in a body paint activity before going swimming?

He reached out an arm, but I shrank back instinctively. His gaze clouded over for a second, then he nodded to himself and withdrew a little.

"I apologise. I didn't want to startle you. How are you faring? Do you need something to hold on to?"

I nodded towards the log which was only a few metres away now. "I'm headed to that log. You can join me, if you wish."

"That is very gracious of you." He smiled. Everything instantly seemed brighter.

I forced myself to look away from him as I swam to the log. It was larger than it had seemed from afar, big enough for several people to hold on to. I grabbed it tight, pushing it against my chest until it was taking some of my weight.

"Ouch!"

A sharp pain shot through my hand.

Fionn was by my side in an instant.

"What is it?" His voice was a strange mix of worry and suppressed anger.

"I think I cut myself on some barnacles. Nothing bad."

"Show me," he growled.

I held out my hand. Water mixed with blood pooled on my palm.

He hissed as if it was him in pain. "I am sorry."

"It's not your fau-"

A wave hit me and I swallowed saltwater. When I'd stopped coughing, I asked him, "Do you know where we are? And how far it is back to the island?"

"Yes, I know, but I am unsure how the distance converts into your units of measurement. Not that it matters. It is too far for you to swim."

Raw indignation rose in me. I hated being underestimated.

"I swim for a living," I snapped. "I can cover any distance you can."

Fionn smiled gently. "I watched you last night. You swim very well indeed, but Kelon brought you far away from the island. You would have to swim all day and even then, it would take a favourable current. You look exhausted already. Your hand is hurt. I would rather you let me carry you."

"Carry me? I doubt that would be much faster." I almost added something along the lines of 'or are you a professional athlete, too'. I didn't like to boast. Only if people underestimated me. Then I was all too happy to show them my medals and titles.

"My species is adapted to life underwater," he began, but I interrupted him.

"Wait a second. *My species?* What the bloody hell are you on about? You're human, just like me."

He grinned. "Trust me. I'm not."

And then he lifted his hair, exposing his neck. On either side of his throat were gashes in his green skin, moving organically like... gills.

"Kelon had those but I thought..." I didn't know how to continue my sentence without sounding ridiculous.

"It's not just that. Here, feel my greenskin."

"Feel your green... skin?"

"Greenskin. One word. It measures the current, makes us more streamlined, aids in navigation. It picks up the smallest movements in the water, which aided our hunting ancestors."

He touched the algae hanging from his left arm, then invited me to do the same.

"No, no, no. Backtrack a little. Species?!"

Fionn shrugged. "I don't know how best to tell you. The dating agency did not give us instructions on how to have this conversation. Maybe they didn't think it would happen so quickly. And it wouldn't have been necessary if Kelon hadn't-"

"Kidnapped me? Yes. Where is he anyway?"

"Unconscious somewhere in the ocean." His voice was bereft of emotion.

"Unconscious?" I shrieked. "But he'll drown! Or he has already drowned!"

"No. Finfolk can't drown. At least not in saltwater."

I stared at him as if he'd gone completely crazy. Or

maybe it was me. I may have been hallucinating the whole thing.

"Elise..." I loved hearing him say my name. "Elise, we are aliens. From another planet."

Crack. That was my sanity breaking into pieces. I laughed hysterically.

Fionn didn't seem to know what to do. "We really are. We've come here in a spaceship because we're searching for females and-"

I couldn't stop laughing. He'd just described every alien romance novel ever.

This couldn't be real. Maybe I was unconscious, having bumped my head on the way into the cave. This could all be a dream.

"I'd quite like to wake up now," I said just before a huge wave hit me from behind. I was pushed against the log, my head underwater. I squeezed my eyes and lips shut, hoping it would be over quickly. But just when cool air hit my face and I breathed in deeply, another wave crashed over me. The log was ripped from my grasp. I was flailing, up turning into down, and I lost all track of where the surface was. I reached out blindly, hoping to find the log again - and a warm hand clasped mine, pulling me to the right.

Which turned out to be up.

I broke through the water's surface, gasping and coughing. Strong hands gripped my hips and pushed me up, above the waves, so I could breathe. I sucked in a few shallow breaths, then looked down at my saviour. Fionn smiled up at me.

His skin glistened in the sun like mother of pearl. The long stretches of algae - what he'd called *greenskin* - fluttered in the breeze as he held me aloft. He treaded water easily even as he had me lifted in front of him.

"Thank you," I rasped. I really needed some fresh water to drink.

"May you let me carry you back to the island now? We can talk on the way. You will have questions."

I stared into his emerald eyes. "You really are an alien?"

"Yes. I am. To you. To me, you are the alien." He smirked. "It's all a matter of perspective."

My head was swirling and it was only partly due to exhaustion.

"Tell me this is real," I asked. "Or better still, tell me that it isn't real and that I'm lying in a coma in a hospital bed. This is too crazy to just accept."

Fionn smiled gently. "Would it help to speak to other Peritans? All the staff on the island know about our true identity. Many of them have had dealings with other alien species in the past."

"Peritans?"

"Ah, that's what we call your species. It's the intergalactic term, even though you seem to have a different word for it."

"Yes. Humans. We're humans."

He grinned. "I will use that term from now on, if it pleases you. Now, can I get you back to the island? I'd rather get there before Kelon wakes up."

His expression clouded over for a moment.

"What is he going to do?"

Fionn's smile disappeared. "Nothing good, I fear."

11

Fionn

Carrying her in my arms was the best feeling in the universe. I swam through the waves on my back, cradling her protectively against my chest. She'd complained at first and I'd let her swim next to me for a while, until she'd given into exhaustion and had finally accepted my help. She was a proud female. I liked that. She knew her strengths, of which she had many.

Her wittleweed scent mixed with the salt of the ocean. I would pay good money for someone who could bottle that scent for me.

As I swam, I told her stories about Finfolkaheem. I doubted she could hear me, exhausted as she was, but I wanted her to hear my voice and know that she was safe.

The tension in my greenskin told me that land was fast approaching.

"We are almost there," I told Elise.

She was half-asleep. Her eyes were red from the salty water and her skin was flushed from sun exposure. Her kind was clearly not made for swimming in the ocean all day. It had taken me a fair while to get us here as I'd taken the calmest route so as not to encounter high waves and dangerous currents. I'd listened out for Kelon, but hadn't heard anything suspicious. If he'd taken the fastest route, however, he might already be back on the island.

I couldn't contact my clutch-brothers while holding Elise and swimming. I just had to hope that they would be ready for whatever was to come.

"When we arrive, there will be other finmen," I warned her. "Remember Cerban and Rainse from last night? They are my brothers."

"All aliens?" she asked weakly.

"Yes. Together with Kelon and the captain, there are twenty-five finmen on board the Tidebound."

She coughed. Maybe I should take her to the medbay. I didn't know enough about Peritan physiology to understand what impact prolonged exposure to saltwater had on their health. Yes, that was a good idea.

Medbay first. Just to make sure. And if she had been harmed... Kelon would not leave this planet alive.

My clutch-brothers were waiting for us on the beach. When they saw us they waded into the water, meeting me where the waves broke over the soft sand.

"How is she?" Rainse asked, concern clouding his voice. For a moment, the acrid taste of jealousy rose in me, but then I relaxed. He was my brother. He wouldn't take her from me. Not like Kelon. He was a threat. Rainse wasn't.

"Mostly exhausted, I think, but I want to get her checked out in the medbay first. Can you make sure the corridors are clear? I don't want her scared by curious finmen lingering about."

Rainse hurried away while Cerban stayed close by my side, a silent, reassuring presence. We walked along the beach, Elise still resting against my chest. She was so light. Peritans were smaller than finfolk, the females especially. Elise was tall for her kind, but she barely reached to my elbow. Carrying her on land was no more trouble than pulling her in water.

"Any sign of Kelon?" I asked Cerban quietly so as not to worry Elise. Her eyes were closed but I could tell she wasn't fully asleep.

"Nothing. And the mood on the Tidebound is shifting. Maggnus was not too pleased to disrupt his meal in order to search for a Peritan. I believe that as soon as Kelon returns, the captain and the crew will bring their demands to him."

"They want their own females."

Cerban clicked his tongue. "Yes. And they don't want to wait. I tried to reassure them that if the dating agency experiment went well, they could all register there. But they wouldn't listen. They thought they were going to a pleasure planet to blow off some steam, scratch that itch. They didn't get that. Now they're desperate for females."

"It's not safe to stay much longer. Should we contact Pam?"

"Maybe. I still hope that the finmen will see sense. Kelon has sway over them. If he intervenes..."

I laughed harshly. "He won't. He's worse than them." I told him how Kelon had abducted Elise and had intended to claim her as his own.

"We should have known. Kelon was always focused on his own needs first, even back in the clutch-school. Remember, he never shared his toys."

"And he'd take the toys of other finboys, not because he wanted them, but out of spite. You are right. We should have known better than to trust him."

The Tidebound came into sight, its camouflage circuits disengaged.

Cerban stopped by the ramp. "I will stay here in case Kelon returns. Call me if you need me."

"Thank you. I hope I won't need to."

I gazed up at the portholes in the side of the ship. Shadows moved behind the glass, curious finmen wanting to know what was going on. I couldn't fault them for it. I'd be the same if I'd been holed up inside the entire time.

"Elise?" I whispered. "We've arrived at our spaceship."

Her eyes flew open. She had to blink a few times. The redness around her eyes was really worrying me now. I had to get her into a medpod as fast as possible.

"Wow," she gasped. "It looks like a giant metal whale."

I stopped for a moment so she could take in the ship and familiarise herself with it. If things worked out as planned, she'd join me on the Tidebound on our way home to Finfolkaheem. The matriarchs would huff and curse and complain, but they would accept a female's choice of mate in the end. I just had to get Elise to choose me.

"I will take you to the medbay to get checked over," I explained as I carried her up the ramp and into the belly of the ship. "Just to make sure you did not come to any harm."

"I'm fine. I just need a shower and my eye drops. I'm used to taking them before and after swimming, but I hadn't planned on being without my mask today. I guess I'm going to have to reimburse the resort for losing their equipment."

I sent more nasty thoughts in Kelon's general direction. "No. It was not your fault. I will tell them that Kelon will be responsible for all costs. And if he refuses to pay, I will do so in his stead."

"You?" I loved the way her lips pursed for that ou-sound. I wanted to lean down and kiss her. But that would be entirely inappropriate. Didn't make me want it any less, though. "It had nothing to do with you. Kelon took me, he ripped off my mask and regulator. You came to help. I'm grateful, but really, you're not responsible for paying for the damage."

I wanted to argue with her, tell her that from now on, I'd take care of anything she needed, but now that we'd entered the Tidebound, her attention shifted to our surroundings.

"It looks so...organic," she muttered, more to herself than to me. "As if parts of the ship were grown. Are those columns made from corals?"

"No, but they were inspired by a similar underwater plant. It makes them light yet incredibly sturdy both in water and in air. About half of the ship is filled with water, which adds to the weight. Everything else is therefore built to be as light as possible."

Her eyes were wide, taking in everything around us. "A spaceship filled with water... that's incredible."

I tried to see the Tidebound with her eyes. I'd been amazed when I'd first set foot on her, but I was used to finfolk technology. It was all new to Elise.

The corridors were rounded and reminded me of lava tubes. We were on the lower deck, which was mostly water-based and held the aquaponic gardens, the training pool, the song chamber and the cargo bay, most of which was air-filled. Underneath us was a deck I'd not set foot on as it was restricted to maintenance and engineering crew only, but I knew it housed the engines as well as a smaller shuttle and escape pods.

I carried Elise into the lift, a brightly lit cocoon that carried us up a deck. If I followed the corridor to the right, I'd get to the crew quarters - half water, half air - and the galley and mess areas, but I turned left, towards the medbay. It was surrounded by empty air-filled quarters reserved for the Peritan females we were hoping to bring home. I didn't mention that to Elise as I explained to her the different rooms we passed. I didn't want to overwhelm her.

"Above us is the upper deck with the bridge and the captain's quarters. It also has a conference room and weapons storage-"

"Weapons?" Elise repeated. "Did you come armed? Are you planning an invasion?"

I chuckled. "No, we're not that kind of aliens. The weapons are only to be used in case we get attacked by space pirates. It's rare in this part of the galaxy, but not impossible."

"Space pirates. I still think I'm dreaming. This is crazy. Next you'll tell me you have a lab where you probe the humans you capture."

"We do not-" I laughed. "Ah. A joke. I hope?"

"I hope so, too. You're not going to probe me, are you?"

"No. The medpod will scan you from top to bottom but unless it finds an injury, the machine won't touch you. Here we are now."

"Where is everyone? It's so empty."

"My brother has made sure that we are undisturbed. I didn't want you to get stared at by strangers. If you do want to meet other finmen later, I will of course facilitate that."

And hate every moment. I wanted to be alone with her, get to know her, talk, admire her beauty, bask in her warmth. I wanted her to realise that we were meant to be together.

But Pam had told us that Peritan females needed time. They did not have mate bonds like we did. They could partner with anyone, multiple times, multiple partners. Some were happy to stay alone forever. As someone who had been denied a mate until I'd taken charge of my own destiny, that thought horrified me. I wouldn't be alone. I could not. But now I had Elise. My pearl.

"Are you going to set me down now?" Elise asked, sounding a bit more energetic than before.

"This is the medbay. Let me bring you to one of the pods. It will be easier if I lay you into it. They were built for larger aliens than you and me. Even I have to climb up a step to enter them."

The light inside the large circular room was gentle on the eyes and lacked the stark brightness I was used from my local medcentre. Five pods were arranged in a semi-circle. We did not have a full-time medic on board, but the second mate, Po'shran, had medical training. The pods could treat most things and rarely required manual intervention.

The closest pod slid open with a gentle hiss when we approached. The inside was all white, with bioluminescent lights circling the edges.

"Are you sure this is fine to use for humans?" Elise sounded worried.

"Of course. I would never expose you to danger. These pods adjust to whatever species enters them. They have access to a vast database. Thanks to the work of the Intergalactic University, there are detailed entries about Peri-, I mean humans."

"Intergalactic University. I feel like every second word you say is more astonishing than the next."

"I have not been to university," I admitted. "I was assigned to guard training after clutch-school."

"Neither have I. There was never time for it. I had to train every single day of the week and I was away all the time for competitions and training camps. Some days I wish I'd decided differently."

"I believe we all do," I said gently. "No matter what species we are. But it does not help to linger on what could have been. We should always focus on the future instead. And I am certain your future will be wonderful, no matter whether you've been to university or not."

I carefully lowered her into the pod. The smart mattress adjusted to her shape, moulding itself around her.

"Ewwww the mattress is moving!" Elise exclaimed. "Is that supposed to happen?"

I laughed at her expression of disbelief. "Don't worry. This is perfectly normal. For some procedures, the patient needs to be held immobile. But don't fear, you can leave the pod at any time. Just let me know if it becomes too much."

I stepped back and activated the pod. The lid slid shut,

only to open again a moment later. An error message flashed on the screen. I cringed.

"Elise... The pod cannot scan through the thick fabric around your body. You will have to undress."

12

Elise

He wanted me to get naked. Bloody hell.

It had been embarrassing enough to be carried by him like a baby. If I'd had even an iota of strength left in me, I would have protested and walked. But he'd been right when he'd said that Kelon had pulled me far away from the island. I'd swum for as long as I could, but at some point, I'd had to admit defeat. I hadn't even been able to see the island yet. My muscles cramped, my skin was frozen despite the wetsuit, my throat sore and my eyes burning. All I'd wanted to do was sleep. It had taken a lot of mental strength to admit to Fionn that I needed his help. I'd always sucked at that. I was a one-woman powerhouse and hated relying on others. But he had simply smiled and taken me into his arms, pulling me along. It had been so different from when Kelon had transported me through the water. With him, I'd been terrified. I'd had no control, I'd been blind, I'd been exposed to his whims.

With Fionn, I'd felt safe. His grip had been protective rather than controlling. He'd made sure that my head was always above water. He'd talked to me while he swam, reassured me, even when I was half-asleep. He'd told me about his world. I wasn't sure if he knew that I'd heard it all. I'd been too weak to reply or even to open my eyes, but I had listened to every word.

His world sounded like a beautiful place. Underwater cities, desolate islands, kelp forests and coral labyrinths. I would love to see it one day. And I wanted to know more about Fionn and his people. Why had they come here? Why did they want to date human women? I didn't know how far his planet was from Earth, but considering scientists hadn't found any planets with life close enough to travel to on rockets, it had to be far, far away.

I felt myself drifting off again. I was so tired.

"Elise. You will need to get out of that suit. Shall I help you?"

I groaned. Just let me sleep.

"Can I have a coffee first?" I mumbled. "So tired."

"I don't know what that is, but here is some water."

A straw was pushed against my lips and I drank greedily. The water had a faint citrus flavour. When I had my fill, I turned my head to the side and opened my eyes. I really didn't want to have to take off my wetsuit.

"Can you just get me to my bed? I don't need a medical exam, I need to sleep. I'll be fine in a few hours once I've recovered from the exhaustion."

My weak, raspy voice belied my words. And Fionn wasn't having any of it.

"I need to know you haven't been harmed. The medpod is the only way to make sure. I will turn around if you if you prefer. I would offer to leave the room but I will have to activate the scan."

Of course he was going to turn his back. I wouldn't let him ogle me.

I tried to sit up. I barely even managed to lift my head before my muscles turned into jelly and I collapsed back onto the mattress. Wow. I hadn't realised just how exhausted I was. How long had I been in the water, fighting the waves and the current?

"Please let me help you." His voice was warm and comforting. "It will be good to get you out of that wet garment and into something dry. I can ask one of my brothers to bring you some new clothes from the fabricator."

"Fabricator?" I asked weakly.

"A machine that can produce any item we require. This vessel is equipped with all the latest tech. It can even create food, although I will always prefer a home-cooked meal. Or a freshly caught fish."

I opened my eyes again just in time to see him grin wolfishly. Now that we were on land and I wasn't distracted by trying to stay alive, I could see that his teeth were a little sharper than mine. Perfect for tearing into prey.

"What do you...your kind eat?"

He chuckled. "I know what you're doing. But I will not let you distract me. I will answer all your questions *while* you get undressed, not before."

I rolled my eyes. He was turning into a mother hen. A very fit mother hen. In the sea, his greenish skin had blended into our surroundings, but here, the colour was striking and alien. His skin ranged from shades of deep emerald to turquoise, with specks of silver dotted around his brows. His hair had seemed almost black in the water, but now that it was starting to dry, it resembled the dark green of fresh seaweed. And then there were those kelp-like growths, what had he called them again? Greenskin.

I couldn't see below his chest from my position in the pod. I was almost glad. It hadn't looked like he was wearing anything around his waist. Did his kind always walk around naked? And what did he look like down there?

I pushed those thoughts far, far away. That was not a direction I was willing to go in. I'd been sent here to date, to find a potential match, but that had been before I'd discovered that Fionn and the others were aliens. Surely, Cleo didn't intend me to date an alien?

"Why are you here?" I asked weakly.

"Because you need a scan."

"No, I mean, why are you on Earth? Why did the dating agency set this up? It makes no sense. Why don't you just look for a woman among your own species?"

That sounded almost racist. I instantly regretted my words.

But Fionn nodded sadly. "There is a good reason, but again, you are delaying the inevitable. May I help you get you out of that very tight garment?"

I knew the wetsuit left very little to the imagination. At least the neoprene was thick enough not to show my nipples through it. After thinking of what he might look like naked, they would be hard and pointy. I hated when that happened. It was embarrassing.

"You can help by unzipping it at the back," I grudgingly conceded. "I will do the rest."

I couldn't quite see that happening yet. I was barely able to hold my head up.

Fionn came closer, watching me cautiously as if searching for hidden injuries. When I didn't move any further, he gently reached for my shoulders and pulled me into a sitting position. In my current state, I had as much core strength as a rag doll. I tried to stay upright, poured all my remaining strength into it, but I wobbled and then I was falling forward and-

His strong hands pulled me back. He kept one hand on my shoulder to steady me while he climbed into the pod, kneeling behind me so I could use him for stability. I gratefully leaned against him. His chest was broad and hard. He smelled of the sea. I closed my eyes and breathed in his scent.

Fionn fumbled with the zip at the back of my neck.

"There's some velcro at the top," I mumbled. A yawn interrupted me. So tired.

"What is.... ah. Yes. That is curious material. It seems inspired by nature."

I didn't have the strength to start a conversation about velcro. I let him hold me upright, let him pull the suit down my arms, and tried not to fall asleep. He paused when he'd managed to free my arms, but when I didn't protest, he pushed the neoprene suit down further, exposing my skimpy bikini top that revealed more than it hid.

I didn't care any more. I just wanted to rest.

"You asked me why we came to your planet," he said in his velvety voice. He continued to undress me while I simply let him do it, listening to his story, swaying at the edge of unconsciousness.

"Generations ago, we wouldn't have needed to. The ratio between males and females was even and anyone who wanted a mate would find one, eventually. But then our climate changed. The warmer the water became, the fewer females were born. In my generation, only one in ten hatchlings was female. And with so few mated pairs, our birth rate is going down every mooncrossing. That's why the Matriarchs implemented a new law just before I was born. They would choose only the strongest, most promising males to pair with females. They would no longer leave our survival to chance. All matches are made based on genetics rather than love." He sighed deeply. "My clutch-brothers and I were not found worthy to have a mate. We were not strong enough."

The sadness in his words touched me deeply. He seemed to be such a kind man and he had proven his strength by rescuing me from the ocean, carrying me through the waves as if it was nothing. Plus he was hot as fuck.

"No partner... ever?" I croaked.

"No. Some males decide to enter a partnership with other males, even if they do not have such a sexual preference. Others save all their credits to spend their holidays on pleasure planets where they can at least satisfy their physical urges. But until recently, we did not think that any other species in the galaxy was compatible with us to have a real mating bond. Sex is possible with many other species, but my brothers and I are looking for more than that. We want the connection that only true mates have."

He pulled the wetsuit down my legs. It landed on the floor with a squelching sound. Good riddance. I wasn't going to wear one again any time soon. And my next trip to the beach would involve a hammock and a book rather than swimming.

"Now the scanner will be able to do its job," Fionn said, but he didn't leave his position behind me. I was secretly glad. I loved how warm and safe I felt leaning against his chest. I could have easily fallen asleep like this.

For some reason, I trusted him. Not just because he'd saved me from Kelon's clutches. He just felt...right.

He sighed. "I don't want to move."

"I don't want you to either," I whispered.

Slowly, he wrapped his arms around me, hugging me. This wasn't sexual. It wasn't so he could feel my boobs against his arms. It was a simple gesture, one of warmth and protection, and I never wanted it to end. His salty scent reminded me of gentle waves rolling over the beach on a summer's day. I smiled as I imagined myself lying on the sand, fully relaxed, happy and content, safe in the knowledge that Fionn was going to watch over me as I slept.

And with that smile on my lips and his scent on every breath I took, I finally surrendered to sleep.

13

Fionn

Her scan results were all within ordinary parameters, save for too much lactic acid in her blood, something the pod quickly rectified. Elise had a few scratches on her face, probably Kelon's doing. My blood boiled as I watched the pod spray a healing salve on the cuts. I would make sure he regretted what he'd done to her.

She was fast asleep when I lifted her out of the medpod. For a moment, I was tempted to carry her into the cabin I shared with my brothers, but it was small and untidy. Besides, the Tidebound was the first place Kelon would return to. I'd checked with Rainse and Cerban. There had been no sign of him yet. It was strange; he shouldn't have stayed unconscious for very long. He would also have been swimming much faster than I had been, carrying Elise, so where was he?

Rainse had said that the atmosphere among the crew was getting darker. It wasn't safe for her to stay on the ship, at least not while Kelon was in power. After what he had done to her, I was tempted to start a mutiny myself. But why would anyone other than my clutch-brothers follow me? We had nothing to offer them...

Or did we?

I carried Elise through the Tidebound and regrouped with my brothers at the ramp. Wordlessly, they walked either side of me, back to the main Peritan building where a group of her kind had gathered.

"What did you do to her?" Paul shouted, barging his way through the crowd. "Put her down!"

Cerban and Rainse closed the distance between us, guarding my flanks. "I have not done anything to her," I said firmly. "She is simply sleeping, exhausted from swimming. I have had her checked over and am taking her to her own bed so that she may rest more comfortably."

Paul's expression softened. "What happened?"

"Kelon, our leader, thought to take her as his female even though it was not her choice. He will be dealt with. If you see him, will you inform me and my brothers as soon as possible? I will call Pam now to see how we shall best proceed."

"If you don't mind, I would like to sit in on this call." Paul didn't look as if he'd take no for an answer. I looked at him with new eyes. He was tall for a Peritan, with thick arms and the look of someone who could handle himself in a fight. Maybe he had not always been a resort manager - or he had been chosen not just for his hospitality qualifications.

"That is agreeable to us. Lead us to her quarters. I want to get Elise comfortable before we call the agency."

Elise woke when I placed her in her bed, but drifted off again as soon as I'd pulled a silky blanket over her. She was smiling in her sleep. I hoped that she would not be plagued by nightmares of what Kelon had done and threatened her with. I could only guard her in life, not in her dreams - no matter how much I wanted to.

We gathered around a small table in her living room. I left her bedroom door open in case she woke confused or disorientated. This time, Paul didn't flinch when I activated my holoband. Pam answered on the first ring.

"What the bloody hell is going on?" She glared at all four of us. The holo projector was not of the best quality and her image was a little washed out around the edges, but her intense stare was enough to make us all feel like finboys being berated by their teacher.

"I called her earlier," Paul admitted. "The agency had to know."

"Yes, we did," Pam snapped. "I can't believe you lost one of your potential matches. You told me you were trustworthy men who knew how to treat a woman. What happened? Where is Elise? I want to know everything or I swear I will jump on the next plane."

"She is sleeping next door," I reassured her, keeping my voice as calm and confident as possible. "She is fine. Exhausted but fine. I will not wake her, but I can show you a video feed if that reassures you."

"She seems to be alright," Paul confirmed.

Pam's expression didn't become any less stern. "What happened?"

I sighed, not sure how best to explain this without her judging us all for one male's behaviour. "She was out for a dive when Kelon took her. Back when we first learned of your planet, his intention was to fly here and abduct some females. When we found your agency and made our arrangement, I thought that I'd managed to persuade him that his was the better way, the right way. But it seems he never believed in waiting to find his mate. Today, he decided to take Elise for himself."

Pam's voice was icy. "And did she consent to this? Did she willingly go with him?"

"She did not. I arrived just in time to pull him away from her. I brought her back to the island and had the medpod check her over. She is unharmed, except for some scratches, but the experience has exhausted her beyond measure. She insisted on swimming by herself for as long as she could, but Kelon had brought her far offshore and Peritans are not made to swim such long a distance."

"Where is he now?"

"We do not know," I admitted. "I left him unconscious in the ocean, but he should have recovered by now."

"Could he be planning to kidnap her again?"

"I will protect her," I snapped, insulted that she didn't think me enough of a protection for Elise.

"That is not what I asked."

Rainse put a hand on my shoulder. "He may. Kelon is a spoilt finman who is not used to having others reject him or ignore his demands. I am worried he might make plans to go after the female again."

"Then you have to find him. Fast. The plane with the other women is still in the air. I will tell them to circle in a holding pattern above the island until I know it is safe for my girls to be there. Paul, I want you to gather all female staff and have them guarded."

Rainse straightened. "I volunteer to guard them." When both Paul and Pam shot him a strange glance, he pushed back his shoulders. "I swear I will not let any harm come to them. I will protect them with my life. My brothers and I are trained warriors. Your Peritan males won't stand a chance against Kelon, but we are stronger than him. Let me do this to atone for our leader's misdeeds."

"He's no leader of mine," Cerban spat. "I will patrol the sea to search for him. But first, we should meet with our ship's captain and crew. If we get them on our side, the Tidebound can easily scan the ocean for Kelon."

I nodded. "I wanted to talk to you about that, Pam. I know that right now, you will find it hard to trust any of us. Kelon has broken not just our, but your trust. However, we need to convince the rest of the crew to switch sides. I see only one way to achieve that other than double their salary, which is not something we have the means for."

Pam grimaced. "I can see where this is going."

"I would like to politely request that all twenty-one finmen are added to your database. I don't want to promise them a female, not if they are of Kelon's stock and don't deserve one. Just the chance that they might find their mate. I believe it might be enough to sway them."

Paul cleared his throat. "Do any of them have a record of mistreating women? Or a criminal conviction? Are they safe to be around women?"

"Kelon's adoptive mother is a matriarch of much power and influence. The Tidebound was chartered with her money. I doubt she would have allowed Kelon to hire anyone without an impeccable record. But I promise we will check, each and every one of them. Even if a few crew members will be ineligible to join your agency's database, it will be enough as long as we have the majority on our side."

"I'm not sure this is what I want," Pam sighed. "But if it means protecting Elise and the other women from harm, I am willing to give it a go. But only under strict conditions. I will personally look at every single man's profile. If I don't like what I see, he will not be added to the Hot Tatties database. And of course they will all have to supply a DNA sample. For this, I will not allow matches based on personality alone. Our genetic algorithm will be the deciding factor."

I bowed my head, relief flooding me. I tried not to show it. "I agree. Thank you, Pam. We really do appreciate it."

"Thank you," both my clutch-brothers said earnestly. They readied themselves to go. Paul also looked as if he was itching to leave and assemble the island's female staff.

"Fionn, I need to talk to you," Pam suddenly said. "Once you have talked to the crew. It is important, but it can wait a little bit."

Again, I felt reminded of clutch-school. Pam would have made a great teacher in another life.

"Of course, Pam. I will call you as soon as I can."

14

Elise

S and was being poured over me, buckets upon buckets. It landed heavily on my naked body, pushing my limbs against the hard ground, trapping me in place. I opened my mouth to scream but more sand rained down on me, filling my mouth, my throat, my lungs. I couldn't breathe, couldn't even scream as I was buried beneath the sand-

"It's alright, Elise. It's just a dream. Wake up. Please, wake up."

I recognised that voice, but it took me a long time to remember. Sleep was sticky and persistent, trying to keep me in its treacherous embrace, but his voice led me back into reality, in a world without sand and fear and pain.

I opened my eyes to find Fionn staring down at me, concern on his perfectly angular face. His features reminded me of a marble statue that had been chiselled by hand but hadn't been polished yet.

"Hi." My throat was dry but a glass of water would soon fix that.

He smiled. "Hi. How are you feeling?"

"Like I've been run over by a lorry. Or been hugged by a giant octopus with anger issues. What time is it?"

"A late morning meal has just been served. You slept throughout the evening and night. I was going to let you sleep for a while longer, but you started thrashing and whimpering. I couldn't watch it. I had to wake you. I hope you will forgive me?"

I laughed. "For waking me from a nightmare? I forgive you. And I thank you." I sat up, relieved that my strength had mostly returned. My arms and legs were sore, and I knew my muscles would be aching for a while, but at least that bone-deep exhaustion had disappeared.

When I remembered why I'd been so exhausted, my mood darkened. "Have you found Kelon?"

"Not yet. But the Tidebound is about to go on a recon flight. He won't be able to hide from her scanners. Would you like to have some breakfast?"

I pushed the blanket off me, only to realise I was still in that skimpy bikini. At least it hadn't slipped while I'd slept.

"Actually, I'd love a shower first. I smell like seaweed."

"A most beautiful scent." Fionn smiled. "I will wait in your living room, if you don't mind."

I was about to ask him to wait outside my suite but then stopped myself. What would be the point? He was already here. He'd seen my body from top to bottom. He had carried me, protected me, saved me. I did not need fake modesty and shame in his presence.

I got up from the bed and swayed for a second as blood rushed to my head. Fionn wrapped an arm around my waist, steadying me.

"I'm fine," I muttered.

"I know. I just... I need to make sure you are alright. It is a deep instinct that I find hard to suppress when I am in your company."

I wanted to lean against him. Feel his warm, strangely textured skin again. Slide my hands over his greenskin, find out what it felt like. But instead, I smiled, stepped away from him and went for a shower.

Fionn looked entirely out of place on that plush sofa. It was too small for this oversized alien. I was taller than most women but next to him, I felt like a child.

He got up as soon as I entered the room. His wide smile made me all warm and fuzzy inside. I could wake up to that any day – no. He was an alien. I was human. This wouldn't work.

Someone had brought two breakfast trays to my suite, laden with both sweet and savoury dishes as well as a giant fruit basket. A pitcher of orange juice stood next to pots of tea and coffee. I was glad I didn't have to leave my private rooms. I wasn't quite ready yet to face other people. For some reason, Fionn didn't count. I was entirely comfortable in his company.

Because Fionn had looked so uncomfortable on the sofa, I grabbed a blanket hanging over one of the armchairs. "Let's have a picnic outside."

For a moment, he hesitated. I thought it was because he wanted to stay inside or because he had better things to do than spend time with me, but then he asked, "What is a picnic?"

I almost laughed in relief. It was just a cultural misunderstanding. I explained the concept to him.

"Why do you prefer to eat on the ground?" he asked, clearly confused about the whole thing.

This time, I did laugh. "I don't even know. I think it's more relaxed than sitting at a table. Maybe I associate picnics with my childhood when us children could be messy and play rather than having to sit still and worrying about table manners. There's a sort of freedom in picnics."

"I am excited to try it. Let me just inform my brothers." He pressed a button on the black bracelet he had around his left wrist. A holographic display appeared above it, hovering in the air like magic. I watched with wide eyes as he scrolled through menus and clicked buttons that didn't actually exist. I wanted to have a go at this technology.

A blue face appeared above his wrist. The man looked vaguely familiar, but my memory of yesterday's events was foggy. Was he the one who had met us on the beach before Fionn had carried me into the spaceship?

"Rainse, we're about to go outside to have breakfast on the beach. Any update on the search?"

"The Tidebound's just taken off. Cerban's on board to oversee the search. Captain Maggnus has been most accommodating after his chat with Pam this morning. I'll update you as soon as I hear something. Po'shran and Liltty have stayed on land to help guard the females."

Fionn sighed. "Hopefully, this will all be over soon and we can focus on the reason we came here."

"Wouldn't that be nice." Rainse grinned. "I have some good news on that front. The plane carrying the other females has landed on a neighbouring island. As soon as Kelon has been found and secured, they will be transported here by boat. The mating game can finally continue."

"Dating, not mating. That would be a very different affair. I don't think the Peritan females want to proceed that quickly."

I suppressed a chuckle. I'd gone on Tinder dates in the past where dating had turned into mating by the end of the evening. None of them had ever resulted in a long-term relationship.

Fionn ended the call and together we carried the food outside. I spread the blanket on a patch of sand close to the veranda and Fionn built us a banquet. I would have preferred to sit further away from the building, but as long as Kelon was still out there, it was better to stay away from the water.

I shuddered.

"What's wrong?"

Fionn must have been watching me.

"Nothing. Just remembered what happened yesterday."

He was by my side in an instant. He hesitated for a second, then put his hands on my shoulders. "I know it will be hard to put that behind you, but please believe me, not all finmen are like Kelon. If his adoptive mother knew how he behaved, she would be ashamed. She'd likely throw him out of the family for good. On my planet, females are treasured. We do not treat them like he treated you."

I craned my neck and looked him straight in the eyes. "I believe you. You have been nothing but kind to me. I almost wish-"

"Yes?"

I wished I hadn't started that sentence. I wanted to tell him that I'd have liked it if I'd had that first dinner with him only. No complications, no confusion, no Kelon. I could have enjoyed the evening and then the memory of it. And maybe there could have been a second date, a third. I could have fallen in love with Fionn.

But as it was, there was so much baggage. Thinking of Kelon still gave me the shivers. I wouldn't sleep easily until he was caught. Could I look at Fionn without thinking of Kelon? How he'd grabbed me, touched me, pulled off my oxygen mask, threatened me?

"You're shaking." Fionn removed his hands from my shoulders. "Are you unwell? What's wrong?"

Again that question.

"I don't... I don't know if I can do this," I whispered.

"Do what?" His tone was gentle yet insistent.

"This. Dating. Us. What the agency wants us to do. We're so different from each other. And-"

"You love swimming. I love swimming. You like fish. I like fish. You are funny and interesting. I like to listen to you. You are small. I am big enough for both of us. You walk on land. I can walk on land as well. You are beautiful. I like to bask in your beauty. You-"

I interrupted him with a laugh. "Stop it. That's not what I meant. Besides, I don't know if I can ever look at you without being reminded of Kelon."

His expression darkened for a moment, then his gentle smile returned. "Kelon is this much shorter than me. His hair is darker and curlier. He has a seventh toe on both feet, a genetic mutation that runs in his family. He-"

"Six toes! You have six toes and fingers. I only just noticed."

"See?" Fionn laughed. "You didn't even notice all the differences between our species. That means they are not important. And really, I'd like to think it's all about what's inside, what we feel in our heart, rather than how many toes we have. Except when we're counting them to be different from Kelon. Then it's very important."

He winked at me.

I chuckled. "You're funny."

"So are you. I told you we're similar. Now, shall we have some of this food? You can explain the dishes to me. I don't know much about human food."

"I'm not familiar with all of these either. I don't know how it is on your planet, but here, every country and region has their own cuisine. I've not been to the Caribbean before, if that is where we are, but I guess we can try these together and figure out what they are."

We sat down on opposite sides of the blanket, the food a barrier between us. I almost wished breakfast was over already so I could find an excuse to snuggle into Fionn. I remembered him carrying me, first in the water, then on land. I'd felt safe in his arms. But was that a reason to go out with him? Was there enough chemistry between us to make this work? And could relationships between humans and aliens even persist?

Wait a minute. The Hot Tatties agency had set this up. Everyone here on the island took being surrounded by aliens in their stride. That made me think that this wasn't the first time they'd set up human women with alien men. I had to talk to Pam.

I told Fionn that I needed a moment alone inside. He probably thought that I had to go to the toilet, because he didn't argue and simply continued to nibble on some fruit.

Back inside, I rummaged for the hotel's tablet and dialled the agency's number. Pam answered on the second ring. I'd met her that day in the office, after I'd talked to Cleo and signed all the forms. When she recognised me, her face lit up.

"Elise! I'm so glad to see you! I was going to give you a ring later but after what happened yesterday, I thought you might need a lazy, undisturbed morning. How are you doing?"

The finmen must have told her about what happened.

"Fine. Mostly. My muscles are sore from all the swimming, but that'll pass quickly. Fionn has been taking care of me."

"Where is he now?"

"Outside. I asked for a moment of privacy because I wanted to speak to you."

A knowing glint appeared in her eye. "I take it you have questions. Before you start, I need you to know that your DNA test results have been added to the database - and there is a match. Usually, I'd pass on this news with more preparation and ceremony, but this case is different."

I froze. My throat was suddenly bone-dry. "Is it one of the finmen?" I croaked.

"Yes."

"Is it... Please tell me it's not Kelon."

She smiled and shook her head. "It is not. His details have been erased from the database and he has been permanently blocked. I have also taken steps to inform the Intergalactic Authority. He tried to abduct an Earth citizen. If you support this going to court, he could be tried as a pirate and people trafficker."

Thank goodness. The relief was like cold rain washing over me, draining away my anxiety.

"Who is it?" I asked.

But I already knew, deep in my heart.

15

Fionn

She was different when she came back. More radiant. More confident. And even more beautiful than before.

I couldn't take my eyes of her. She'd put on a simple flowy dress that accentuated her curves. I watched as she ate, listened as she explained the various dishes to me, laughed at her jokes. She was so perfect it hurt.

I was sure now. She was mine. My mate. All doubt had vanished.

Before the matriarchs had restricted normal dating, there had been a simple test for finmen to find their true mate. All you had to do was to hold your greenskin against hers. If you weren't mates, you'd get a slight

tingle, almost uncomfortable. But if you were mates...
I'd heard it described as an almost spiritual experience.

Nowadays, this rarely ever happened. Matches were
made for genetic potential, for keeping our species
alive, not for love. I was sure that some of the rich and
powerful still got to choose their mates for themselves,
but not us, not normal finfolk. Males had to stand
before the Matriarchal Panel and females had to accept
whoever they were assigned. It was no way to live. I
hated that my kind had to resort to such methods in
order to survive. In one way, I could understand why
the matriarchs had designed this law. For the good of
the species. But for a finman like me who, if they had
their way, would never have a mate, never find love,
never lie in the arms of a female - it was torture.

"What are you thinking of?" Elise suddenly asked.

"You." Always.

"Well, then we match because I was thinking about you
as well." She smiled and pushed her plate away. "When
you registered with the dating agency, what was your
plan? Long-term, I mean. Did you want to return to
your planet? Fin..."

"Finfolkaheem."

"Originally, we wanted to find some females and take
them back home. To be honest, we hadn't thought much
about it. When we set off, we half expected the story

from our Archives to turn out to be a fairytale. We didn't dare to hope. Even when we made contact with the dating agency and got confirmation that Peritans did exist and that there might be a way to find mates for ourselves, it felt like a dream. I think I always assumed that I would return to Finfolkaheem, but that was not based on rational thought. I don't know what the matriarchs would do to us if we brought a group of Peritan females with us. Would they accept you? Would they want to know if our two species could have offspring together? Would they commission experiments on you?"

My greenskin tightened at the thought. I would never let that happen. Elise would always be safe with me. Even if I had to protect her from my own people.

"Maybe we should stay here."

Her words made my heart stop.

We.

Us.

Together.

Did she mean that? Or had it been just a slip of the tongue?

"Elise... are you saying that you could imagine being with me?"

Everything inside me froze. Time slowed into a sticky

syrup that refused to flow faster. Her silence was an eternity, until-

"You are my match." Her words were quiet but certain. "Pam told me just now. According to her genetic test, we are a match."

Time became a rippling current that swept me away. I couldn't breathe. Couldn't believe it.

"Fionn?"

I took a deep breath to steady myself. "I... I didn't think it would happen so soon. Pam didn't give us much hope. Just because our ancestors had found mates on Peritus didn't mean that we would achieve the same. But here you are, my mate. My Elise."

I wanted to touch her, kiss her, but the mountains of food still separated us. Elise's gaze also flicked to the plates between us. She must have been thinking the same thing. I hoped.

I swept my arm across the blanket, pushing all the dishes into a messy heap on the side. Elise - my mate - gave me a wide-eyed look, then laughed.

"I guess that's one way of tidying up. What are we doing now?"

"Now, I will kiss you."

I breached the distance between us and knelt before her, cupping her face. Her skin was soft and warm. The scratches on her cheeks had faded but I could still see where Kelon had injured her. He would pay. I would make him pay.

Gently, I lowered my lips to hers. It was instinctual.

I had never done this before, but I had watched it often enough to know what to do.

The moment our lips met, my old life ended and my future began.

She tasted of everything I'd been missing. Her lips were soft yet strong as she met my kiss with the same passion I felt. Her hands snaked around my back, pressing me against her, while our tongues began to dance. I stopped breathing. Nothing mattered but her taste, her warmth, her presence. I drowned in her kiss until all my layers peeled away; the guard, the clutch-brother, the rejected male, the hopeless warrior.

She clung to me, wrapping her legs around my waist. My cock came to life, hard and strong, desperate for attention. She must have felt him press against her belly, but she did not recoil. If anything, she pulled me even tighter against her small body.

When we finally broke apart, both of us were breathing heavily. Her lips and cheeks were flushed, her pupils dilated. I loved seeing her like that. I'd had that effect on her, nobody else. My cock tented the Peritan-style shorts I was wearing in her honour, and for a moment, her attention flicked down there, but she didn't comment.

"Thank you," I said breathlessly. "Thank you so much."

She cocked her head to the side. "Are you thanking me for a kiss?"

"Is that not done amongst Peritans? We are taught to thank a female for any and all physical attention."

"No, I don't think we have a rule about that on Earth. But please keep doing it. I like it."

I smirked. "Does that mean there will more kisses I can thank you for?"

"I think that can be arranged. Where did you learn to kiss like that? I've never... it was spectacular."

Her praise hardened my cock even further. I would have to find a quiet moment to take care of him - unless Elise... No, this was not the right time. Kelon was still out there. I couldn't give in to my urges and fantasies only to then be surprised by him at the worst possible moment.

A deep buzzing sound far away made me straighten. The Tidebound was on the move. Hopefully, they would find Kelon before the midday meal. He could have swum a fair distance since his disappearance, but the Tidebound had advanced scanners that would reach deep into the sea. He could not hide from us for long. And once he was back on this island, we would make sure he never had an opportunity to harm a female again.

"Do you want to stay here for a bit longer?" I asked Elise. "Or we could go for a walk? Or a swim?"

I had to force myself to suggest these things. I wanted to keep her locked into her suite where it was safe, where I could guard and protect her. But I knew better than to expect her to sit there like a caged avian. She was a female used to being active. She wouldn't enjoy being cooped in, despite the danger to her life.

"I don't think I'm quite ready for a swim yet. I hate to admit it but my muscles still feel like I've swum a marathon. How about we try the hammock? It looks big enough to fit us both. You can tell me more about life on Finfolkaheem and I can explain some human traditions to you." She pulled her small communicator device from her pocket. "I can show you pictures of my home, where I come from. And my parents."

Parents! For some reason, we had not talked about her family yet. Guilt bubbled up in me. I should have been more interested in her life, asked her more questions. I had to show her just how interested I was in her.

"What are their names? Are you close?"

"They were called Stacey and Ron. But they're no longer with us. They were killed in a car accident five years ago."

I didn't say anything. I simply pulled her closer, wrapping her in my arms until the world could no longer hurt her.

She sighed. "I wish you could have met them. They always supported me, no matter how cracked up my ideas were. One year, I decided I'd become an Arctic explorer. We didn't have much money at the time, but dad bought me a ridiculously oversized ski jacket in a charity shop and then drove us up to the Cairngorm mountains. There's a wild reindeer herd there, and we got to visit and feed them. On the way home, we stopped at the Highland Wildlife Park to see the polar bears." Elise sniffed. A single tear rolled down her cheek.

I wiped it away before licking my finger. Salty. Like the sea.

"I am so sorry," I whispered. I ran my fingers through her short, silky hair, wishing there was something I could do for her. Grief was a terrible beast. No matter how much you thought you had it under control, it could never be fully tamed. And it always broke from its chains when you least expected it.

"I've had time to process it. But it still hurts. I don't think that will ever pass." She took a deep breath. "What about your parents? Are they still alive?"

"I don't know. We are not raised by our biological parents on Finfolkaheem. Finbabes are given to the hatchery where they are assigned to clutches of three to four. Cerban and Rainse are my clutch-brothers. We are not related genetically, but we grew up together as brothers."

"Was it always that way?" she asked softly.

"No. The system was set up so females could focus on producing more offspring for the endurance of our species. By not having to care for their finbabes, they are free to put all their energy into procreating." I hated how detached and clinical I sounded. I'd never liked the idea of having to give away my offspring, should I ever have a mate. I wanted my finbabes to grow up with us, as a family, not raised by an army of carers and teachers.

"Sometimes, a matriarch will adopt a finbabe," I continued. "If they see potential in a child, they may be raised to become a leader or politician or a future matriarch. That's what happened to Kelon."

Elise snorted. "They made a bad choice with him."

"I agree. He was given every opportunity my clutch-brothers and I can only dream of, but look at what he did-"

Suddenly, a shudder went through Elise. She stiffened, her eyes wide.

"What is happening?" she whispered, before she dissolved into thin air.

16

Elise

My body was torn apart, scattered in all directions, before I was put together again in a flash of light and pain.

I staggered, collapsed, landing in a heap on a cold metal floor. It took me a second to remember how to breathe.

"ELISE FARROW."

The voice boomed from all around me.

I looked up, blinking against the bright light surrounding me, and forgot how to breathe again. I was in a spaceship, that much was clear. Before meeting Fionn and the other finmen I would have questioned if this was real or just a dream - but I had learned a lot in the past few days. My horizon had expanded beyond belief.

The room was oval, as big as a house, with metallic walls that pulsed with an ethereal glow, and a floor that was shimmering like quicksilver. I wouldn't have been surprised if I'd suddenly sunk through the metal. The room was split in two halves by a giant glass wall. On the other side stood a figure. With the way the light fell on him, I could only make out his silhouette, no details, but I recognised him right away.

Kelon.

I jumped to my feet, swaying at first as I found my balance, but anger at the alien who'd abducted me gave me new strength.

Kelon turned around slowly. His eyes found mine and he smiled. The malice in his gaze made my gooseflesh rise. I didn't want to be anywhere near this man. The glass separating us suddenly didn't feel like enough protection.

"What-" I snarled, but the disembodied voice interrupted me.

"THE HEARING OF THE INTERGALACTIC AUTHORITY IS CONVENED. SUBJECTS: KELON SHELL-CLUTCH OF ROUSSAY; ELISE FARROW OF PERITUS. WITNESSES ARE PRESENT."

"I didn't agree to—" Kelon began.

"YOU DO NOT CONTROL THESE PROCEEDINGS."

He flinched. I breathed in slowly, steadying myself. He was not in charge here. This was neutral ground. I was safe.

"ELISE FARROW'S MEMORIES HAVE BEEN LAWFULLY ACQUIRED AND VERIFIED."

What the fuck?

The wall to my right flashed brightly, then turned into an image. Underwater, bubbles floating through the murky sea. Fast movement. Shadows flicking at the edge of the screen. This could have been filmed anywhere, but I knew in my heart that this was what I'd seen when Kelon had dragged me through the water at a speed only his kind could achieve.

And yes, there was my hand, gripping the tube connecting the regulator to my oxygen tank. More shadows. Kelon's body, huge and scary. His hand clawing at the camera - at my face. Breaking the surface, sunlight streaming down on us, water drops flying everywhere, and then his face, a mask of greed and delight. He loved seeing me helpless like that. He enjoyed inflicting fear and pain.

But I didn't want to watch this without commentary. I needed to make my voice heard.

"Kelon grabbed me," I said loudly. "He didn't check if I was breathing. He didn't check *anything*."

"THE RECORD REFLECTS THIS."

I didn't want to see it. But when I turned my head away from the screen, the wall opposite flashed and began to show the same memory from Kelon's perspective.

To Kelon, I had looked small and vulnerable. He watched Maelis and me swimming down towards the cave entrance. He waited for her to have a slight lead, then he rushed me, wrapping his arms around me, crushing me against his chest. And then he swam and swam, far away, never checking on my wellbeing. I could have been unable to breathe and he wouldn't have noticed. That by itself told me everything I needed to know.

Kelon smoothed his hair, trying to appear bored. "You are dramatizing a rescue."

A rescue? What an arse.

"I would like to speak," I said, louder. "I want to set the record straight."

"PROCEED."

I stepped closer to the glass so Kelon would have to look at me. "Kelon took me against my consent. He never asked. He didn't give me any warning. He just took."

Kelon leered at me. "You're just saying that because I'm an alien. If I were Peritan, you would have accepted me."

I scoffed. "It has nothing to do with your species and everything with your behaviour. Fionn... From the first moment, he asked before he touched me. He called the Hot Tatties agency instead of breaking rules. He put me first."

My hands were shaking. I waited for the genderless voice to react. The silence felt like the held breath before a dive.

A new rectangle flickered into life—*another* window, this time a live feed. Fionn. His face filled the projection, jaw set, shoulders squared, the dark fall of his hair pulled back. Behind him: Captain Maggnus and two crew, tense but present.

"WE HAVE BEEN PROVIDED WITH EVIDENCE FROM A RELIABLE WITNESS."

For a moment, I expected Fionn to appear in the room, but instead, a new screen flashed to life, showing another large finman.

"I am Captain Maggnus," he said in a deep, polished voice. "This is an internal bridge log captured at 03:12 ship-time the sunpass before landfall."

An audio recording played, echoing through the room. Kelon's voice was loud and clear.

"That's why I want to keep our stay on Peritus as short as possible. Land, grab some females, test if we're compatible, grab some more females, leave."

"YOU ATTEMPTED TO ABDUCT A PROTECTED BEING," the disembodied voice said tonelessly. "WITHOUT PERMISSION FROM THE INTERGALACTIC AUTHORITY NOR THE ASSOCIATED AGENCIES."

"Protected... As if. She *wants* to be with a finman," he scoffed. "Peritans don't even-"

"Stop saying Peritans like we're insects," I snapped. "And I'm here because you dragged me under the water."

His lip twitched. "You were intrigued enough by our world."

"Not by *you*," I said. I didn't raise my voice. "By Fionn."

He didn't reply, just glared.

I stared back at him, finally facing him without fear. "Why me, Kelon? Why choose the moment when I was diving? You could have asked to talk on land."

He worked his jaw. "Because you were there, swimming where I was swimming. And asking takes *time*."

There it was. Not romance. Not fate. Logistics.

"And were there going to be others?" I pressed. "Maelis? Any woman on the island? Just items on a list? Are we just objects to you?"

He didn't answer. His silence was answer enough.

"THE INTERGALACTIC AUTHORITY HAS EVALUATED THE MEMORIES AND WITNESS REPORTS. WE HAVE COME TO A DECISION."

My heart beat against my chest during their dramatic pause. Come on, tell me. What was going to happen?

Pam had mentioned that Intergalactic Authority. She'd said she'd reported Kelon's behaviour to them. I hadn't expected them to act this quickly, however? Had they been on Earth already? Or had I been transported into space?

I shuddered at the thought of how far from home I might be. I hadn't been able to say goodbye to Fionn. I'd just disappeared, no warning. He must be frantic with worry. Maybe he'd assume that this was Kelon's doing. My anger only increased when I imagined the pain Fionn would be going through. This was all Kelon's fault.

"KELON SHELL-CLUTCH OF ROUSSAY IS HEREBY BANNED FROM EVER COMING WITHIN TEN LIGHTYEARS OF PERITUS. HE WILL BE BANNED FROM ALL PLEASURE PLANETS AND MOONS. HE WILL BE REPORTED TO THE FINFOLKAHEEM

AUTHORITIES WHO MAY INSTIGATE FURTHER INVESTIGATIONS AND PUNISHMENTS. HE WILL ALSO PAY COMPENSATION TO ELISE FARROW IN THE AMOUNT OF A QUARTER OF HIS ACCUMULATED WEALTH AS WELL AS THE OWNERSHIP OF THE VESSEL 'TIDEBOUND'. HE WILL BE TRANSPORTED TO FINFOLKAHEEM IMMEDIATELY."

I needed a moment to process what had just happened. Kelon was being sent home like an unruly boy excluded from school. And I'd been given compensation. Credits had to be money, not that I had any idea how finfolk money translated to British Pounds. And... the spaceship? Was it really mine?

That couldn't be. I had no idea how to fly one. And where would I even park it?

Before I could ask the alien voice what all this meant, icy cold ran over my skin once more. I dissolved...

... and then I was on the beach, voices yelling all around me.

Strong arms lifted me from the sand and then I was cradled against his broad chest, his sea salt scent all around me. Fionn.

"Elise," he breathed. "Elise."

"I'm back. I'm okay."

He nuzzled my neck, burying his face in my hair. I heard him breathe in deep, as if he needed to smell me to reassure him that I was real. Poor guy.

"Are you hurt?" he asked with suppressed urgency.

"No, I'm fine. But you're about to break my ribs if you keep hugging me like this."

He instantly loosened his grip. As much as I wanted him to hug me, he also didn't know just how strong he was compared to me.

"It was the Intergalactic Authority," I explained, looking up at his puzzled face. "They put Kelon on trial. He's gone. They're sending him back to your planet. He's never going to return here. And... for some reason they gave me the Tidebound."

His eyes widened. "You got Kelon's spaceship?"

"Yes, along with a quarter of his money."

He stared at me for another long moment, then the lines on his forehead eased and he erupted into laughter.

"That's brilliant! You've just become one of the richest people on your planet!"

"I'm rich?" I felt numb. I didn't know what to say or do.

"Kelon himself didn't do much to accumulate wealth, but he is the sole heir to his adoptive mother's estate. She has been transferring millions of credits to him over many mooncrossings to avoid taxes. He boasted about it during our journey here. Let's wait until the IA completes all the formalities, but if you're lucky, you might even own property on Finfolkaheem."

"No way."

Fionn grinned. "Kelon is obsessed with living the luxury life. The IA made an informed decision. This will hurt him much more than being banned from Peritus."

"And all pleasure planets."

He laughed even harder. "Oh, poor Kelon. Now he will have to stroke his own rod rather than pay a prostitute to do it. And I bet his adoptive mother won't be happy. She might finally give up on him."

He carried me to the hammock. I didn't tell him to let me walk on my own two feet. I enjoyed being in his arms too much. That didn't mean that I couldn't be a strong, independent woman at other times. But right now, I needed to feel, smell, taste him.

"I do not believe this contraption will carry both our weight," Fionn said with a quizzical look at the hammock. It seemed big enough to me, but I didn't know what finmen weighed.

"I suppose... my bed is definitely big enough for the both of us."

He didn't reply. He just stared at me.

Had I been too forward? Had I made a mistake?

But then he growled, "Oh, my sweet little Peritan. Are you sure you are ready for this?"

No?

I knew that this wasn't a one-night stand. Fionn wasn't that kind of guy. He'd come to Earth to find a mate, a woman who would stay with him forever. Who would love him, cherish him, maybe start a family.

Could I be that woman?

"I want you," I said, barely a whisper. My throat was suddenly tight. "But will this work?"

"I will find it hard to blend in among Peritans," he said, misunderstanding me completely. "But we could live on this island, where people are used to aliens. Or find a similar place. Buy our own island. Or I could take you to Finfolkaheem and-"

"I meant, will you fit?" I interrupted. My cheeks burned.

His eyebrows shot up. "Will I...? Oh." He laughed. "There are mentions in the Archives of offspring between finmen and Peritan females. The couple I first read about, Ma'vel and Jonet, had children together. They stayed on your planet, blending in perfectly with the local population, so I assume they must have looked more like Peritans than finfolk. I wonder if today, some of their descendants are still alive." Fionn smiled at me.

"Maybe you are one of them. It would explain why you are such an excellent swimmer. And why the two of us found each other."

I pushed that thought aside. Something to dwell on later. Maybe Pam could test my DNA for it. But now, all I wanted to do was claim Fionn for myself.

"Bed," I commanded. "Now."

With a triumphant smirk, he carried me back to the resort as fast as he could, sand flying all around us. He burst through the veranda doors, only for us to be face to face with Cerban, Fionn's brother. The alien looked at us with bemusement and surprise.

"You could have told us you found her. Was it the IA as I'd suspected?"

"Yes. Kelon has been captured and will not return here. You can stop the search. Tell the crew to take the day off and relax. Also speak to the Peritans, please, and let them know what's going on. Now leave us."

Cerban laughed. "Don't worry, brother. I don't want to watch this. I will wait until I find my own female." He turned his attention to me. "I am honoured to have you join our family."

The finman left with a smile on his lips. Fionn didn't waste any more time and carried us into the bedroom. The bed had been made in my absence. The windows were open and the curtains were blowing in the breeze.

Someone had arranged a beautiful bouquet of flowers on the nightstand. Did everyone know that Fionn was my match?

"Sorry for that interruption," Fionn said as he gently lowered me onto the cool silk sheets. "Cerban was right, I should have called him the moment you arrived back on that beach. But now that he knows, he can deal with everyone else and leave us in peace. You deserve it. Maybe I should let you have a nap to make sure you're fully recovered-"

"No way," I interrupted. "I'm not going to wait any longer. I want you. Here, now. If you want me."

"Want me?" Fionn laughed. "I've never wanted anything more. I have travelled across the stars to find you, Elise. I knew that you were mine the instant I first heard your voice. There may have been a screen between us, but it could not hide your beauty nor your inner spark. I didn't need Pam and her tests to confirm that we are mates. I have always known."

He gently pushed the dress over my shoulders. It slipped down my arms, exposing my naked breasts. I hadn't bothered with a bra after the shower this morning. The fabric pooled around my waist, cool against my heated skin. Fionn's eyes darkened, his greenskin trembling as if mirroring the shiver running through me. He touched me reverently, fingertips almost hovering over my skin, as though I might vanish if he was too rough.

Up close, he seemed even larger, his broad shoulders and muscled chest framed by the greenskin that clung like kelp to his ribs and hips. He cupped my cheek, careful, as though I might startle.

"You're so small, so soft," he murmured, thumb tracing the curve of my jaw. The coolness of his touch made me tremble, though heat unfurled low in my belly. I wanted him so much.

"I don't feel small with you," I whispered, sliding my hands across the hard planes of his chest. His gills flared when I reached the perfect lines leading to his hips.

His lips curved, revealing the faint point of sharp teeth, a predator's smile turned gentle just for me. "Elise... my mate."

He lowered himself, pressing me into the silk sheets, his hair falling around us in an ink-black curtain. The scent of salt and sea wrapped around me, intoxicating, familiar yet utterly new. His weight, his heat, his alien strangeness - all of it was mine.

I pulled him down to me, claiming his mouth. His kiss was nothing like human kisses - hotter, hungrier. His taste filled me, intoxicating, like diving into deep water and knowing you'd never come up for air. His sharp teeth scraped against my bottom lip, before his tongue teased away the sting, soothing, then diving deeper.

My legs parted around him, and he pressed closer, his harness pushing against me with urgency. One large hand cradled my hip, the other exploring lower, fingertips testing, stroking, making me moan into his mouth. Every touch was reverent yet filled with a hunger barely held in check.

"Fionn," I gasped, desperate now. "Please... I don't want slow."

"I want to explore your body." His voice was deliciously husky. "I want to get to know every part of you. Worship you from top to bottom. But now, today, I will lay claim to you."

His fingers reached my core, sneaking beneath my panties. He parted my lips before pushing one thick, calloused finger inside of me. I gasped, spreading my thighs wider. If that was his finger, what would his dick feel like? What if he didn't fit? I needed him so much. I would take it no matter how painful, but I could only stretch so wide.

"You are so tight," he breathed. "I need to prepare you first."

He removed his hand from between my legs, leaving me empty and bereft. I groaned with disappointment at the sudden change.

"Patience, little one."

Fionn pulled the dress down my legs and threw it onto the floor. He rubbed me through my wet panties, eliciting a string of moans, then ripped them apart.

I wanted to reprimand him for destroying my lingerie, but suddenly his mouth was between my legs, hot breath against my swollen lips. When his tongue curled around my clit, I almost came there and then. My fingers clawed at the sheets, searching for something to steady me, as he pushed his tongue deep inside me.

Fuck.

His bottom teeth pressed against my clit, teasing me with the promise of bites and nibbles. He gripped my thighs with his massive hands and pulled them apart further. His tongue did things I had no words for. Flicks, deep dives into my inner sanctum, swirls and pushes, driving me further and further into ecstasy. I moaned without control over the sounds I was making.

He stopped for a breath, and I looked down just in time to see him resurface from between my legs, his face covered in my wetness, his pupils dilated, his skin a darker shade it had been before.

"Delicious," he growled, voice rough, primal. His tongue flicked over his lips, lapping up what I'd given him. "I could feast on you for days."

"Fionn," I whimpered, half-plea, half-demand. I was shaking, trembling with need. "I can't... I need more."

His smile was dark and knowing as he crawled up my body, dragging his mouth across my stomach, my breasts, until he kissed me again. I tasted myself on his lips. The intimacy of it sent another shiver through me.

"Mine," he whispered against my mouth. "You'll always be mine."

"And you are mine. Now fuck me."

He kissed me one last time. "Gladly."

He straightened and I saw him for the first time. Fuck. He was huge. A dark shade of turquoise that turned a shimmering silver at the bulging head. Below, three balls rather than two, the silky skin textured like scales. He took his cock into his hand and the skin *rippled*. I blinked. Ridges moved beneath the surface, up and down like waves on the beach. That was going to feel incredible inside me.

"Like what you see?" He ran his hand along his cock and the ripples moved faster.

"That's incredible."

"I take it Peritan males look different?"

"You can say that again. Do you have control over those...ripples?"

"A little. But I know that as soon as I bury myself inside you, I will lose all control. You are beautiful, Elise. You smell like the most delicious dessert in the galaxy. And now I will claim you."

He pushed my thighs apart again and positioned himself between them, his cock pushing against my entrance.

"Ready?" he asked. I knew this was my last chance. He was holding back for my sake.

"Do it. Fuck me." I barely recognised my own voice.

The first push took my breath away. He stretched me wide, filling me inch by inch, until the burn blurred into a fullness that made my back arch off the sheets. I cried out, but then his hands were on my breasts, twirling my nipples, distracting me from the pain.

"Don't move," I gasped. "Give me a moment to adjust."

He leaned over me, a hulk of a man, and kissed me. It was not a gentle kiss. He claimed me with his tongue, plundering my mouth, until we were breathless and his taste filled my mouth.

I ran my hands over his back, hesitating when I got to the place on his flank where skin turned to greenskin.

"Touch it," he whispered hoarsely. "Please."

Gingerly, I slid my fingers along the smooth strips of skin. They were slightly wet. If I'd had my eyes closed, I would have assumed I was touching kelp.

Fionn groaned. "Do... not... stop."

He continued the kiss while I stroked his greenskin, marvelling at how smooth and slick it was. It shivered beneath my touch, the most alien part of him. He'd said it could sense currents in the water. Did it sense what I felt for him?

Fionn began to move in me, slow strokes at first, then picking up speed. I was stretched to the brink, but I was so wet that I was no longer in pain. I knew he was holding back. He was fully controlled, scared to let go. For this first time, I accepted that. But once he understood that I wasn't breakable, that he would not hurt me, I would demand that he give up all control and surrender to the desperate need driving us both.

"Too much?" he panted. His green eyes burned into mine, desperate and tender all at once.

I shook my head fiercely. "Don't you dare stop."

Pleasure built in relentless waves. My cries filled the room, unrestrained, shameless. He drove into me harder, faster, chasing me to the edge. His fingers found my clit, stroking in time with his thrusts, while I massaged his greenskin. His hand cupped my breast, flicking my nipple just the way I liked it, and I shattered around him with a scream.

He followed me over the edge a moment later, roaring my name as he spilled inside me, his body convulsing against mine. His sharp teeth closed on my shoulder in a primal claim, not breaking skin but sending another jolt of ecstasy through me.

The ripples around his cock were relentless, driving me from one shattering climax to another, while I screamed and swore and revelled in bliss. I was surfing the wave and he was there, next to me, holding me, whispering to me until I reached the shore and could breathe again.

We collapsed together in the tangle of silk sheets, both shaking, breathless. His greenskin stuck to my sweaty skin, connecting us. It shuddered softly every time he took a breath.

Fionn kissed me softly, reverently. I was limp, barely able to return the kiss. Still floating in post-orgasm bliss.

"Elise," he murmured, voice hoarse. "You're my mate. My future. My everything."

17

Fionn

The meeting was too formal for my taste. Elise shifted in her seat, clearly just as uncomfortable as me.

Captain Maggnus was opposite us, flanked by the first and second officer. He was a huge male, not the smartest, but he carried himself with a natural authority. Pam was joining via holocall, while my brothers and Paul, the resort manager, were seated to my right.

We'd already talked to the IA earlier in the day to finalise Elise's compensation claim. The Tidebound was now officially hers, as was an intergalactic bank account with more credits than she could spend in a lifetime. She'd mentioned something about donating to a charity that helped children from unprivileged backgrounds learn to swim. I would support her no matter what she decided to do with the credits.

"Kelon paid our salaries for the journey, but not for the prolonged stay here," the captain continued his argument. "We've now been here for six Peritan sunpasses. If you want us to stay for much longer, you will have to pay us."

Pam cleared her throat. "You are free to leave at any time, but I will not send female matches to Finfolkaheem. All first encounters have to happen here or elsewhere on Earth, under controlled circumstances. We've learned our lesson with Kelon. From now on, there will be more of an agency presence at these dating events."

I knew the captain and almost the entire crew - save two who had made comments along Kelon's line of thinking - were waiting to find matches in the agency's database. It was pure greed that he wanted to be paid while also getting the opportunity to find a mate.

"I can pay you," Elise sighed. I thought she'd bowed to Maggnus' pressure, but then she added, "As long as you are prepared to transport anyone who is part of the dating agency or who is a potential match to the island and back."

Captain Maggnus frowned. I bet he'd imagined an easy life for himself, lying by the beach and exploring the local ocean all day while on full pay, rather than having to do actual work. But then he inclined his head.

"That will change of course when I have found my own mate."

Elise smiled. "Of course. Same goes for anyone in your crew. They can all get a long holiday when Pam finds a match for them. And if there are any happy couples by the end of this process, you and your crew can decide whether you want to continue to work for me or settle somewhere else."

"What if we want to return to Finfolkaheem?" Po'shran, the second mate, asked.

Elise exchanged a look with me. "Fionn and I plan a trip there some time in the future. I want to see your planet before we decide where to settle. Anyone who wants to come with us can. But first, I need the Tidebound to fly me home. There is a place I want to show to Fionn."

We'd waited for nightfall. I was dressed head to webbed toe in bulky black clothes and had covered my head with a cap that threw shadows on my face. Even so, anyone who came close would see that I wasn't human, but it would do for this short excursion.

Elise had brought me to a large, square building at the edge of her city. The Tidebound was parked in a special part of the airport that the Hot Tatties agency had chartered when they'd first encountered an alien species. One of Pam's employees had driven us here in a four-wheeled vehicle with blacked out windows to make sure I didn't cause a riot. I'd had my face plastered to the window, trying to take in as much of Elise's world as possible.

It was so different here compared to the tropical island. Grey buildings, narrow streets, flickering lights, noise drifting to us from all directions, and a smell difficult to describe. And so, so many humans. I'd thought it impossible to find a quiet spot where I wouldn't be discovered, but Elise had chosen well.

"Ready?" she asked, her hand already on the door handle.

"I'm very intrigued."

She'd not told me where she was taking me, just that this was a place that held great importance to her. I would have followed her to the end of the world.

We stepped out of the car and I instantly sought Elise's side. Not because she needed protection, but because I couldn't bear to be away from her. She took my hand and together we walked up a flight of stone steps. Elise had the keys to the large glass doors. As soon as she opened them, a strange smell made me sneeze.

"Chlorine," she laughed. "During the day when these doors are open, you can smell it from all around here."

I followed her through the dark building, along a corridor and through rows of tiny rooms that seemed too small to spend time in until we came to another set of glass doors. The hall beyond was dark, but I could still make out the pool of water in its centre.

I scented the air, searching for the smell of the sea beneath the sting of the chlorine, but there was no salt, no kelp.

"Freshwater," I muttered.

"Yes. Welcome to my pool. This is where I spent most of my adult life - and childhood, to be honest. It's an Olympic size pool, which is why a lot of athletes come here to train. I was lucky that my parents' home wasn't far so I could come here any time I liked."

I wasn't too sure about swimming in this pool. On the Tidebound, we had a pool to train in and keep our muscles from wasting in the weightlessness of space, but it had been recreated in the spirit of the ocean. Saltwater that was constantly filtered, artificial waves, kelp and seaweed growing at the bottom, even a small school of fish to filter the water. This was as far removed from that pool as possible. Yet this place was where Elise had found her passion. I loved it just because of that. If she hadn't been a swimmer, would we ever have met?

"Would you like to swim a few lengths?" Elise asked.

No, I didn't want to enter this water - but for her, of course I would.

"I would love to."

Still holding my hand, she led me into the dark hall. Only the emergency lights were on, glimmering high above us.

Elise peeled off her clothes until she was down to a sleek swimsuit that hugged her curves. She looked over her shoulder at me, a mischievous spark in her grey eyes.

"Coming in?"

I wanted to say no. This wasn't my element, not truly. The chlorine stung my nose, the stillness felt unnatural without the pull of tide or current. But this was *her* place, her sacred ground. For Elise, I would swim in fire if she asked.

She dove gracefully into the pool, her body cutting through the surface with barely a splash. Even without the sea, she moved like she was born for water. My chest ached with pride as I watched her glide away, her form as fluid as any finfolk's.

I stripped down and followed her in. The water clung differently to my skin, too thin, too clean, but the moment Elise surfaced, laughing, I forgot everything else. She swam back to me, wrapping her arms around my neck.

"Not so bad, is it?" she teased.

I caught her waist, tugging her close until our bodies pressed together beneath the surface. "If you're here, it's perfect."

She kissed me, or maybe I kissed her. Suddenly, I didn't care about the chlorine or the missing waves. I was with Elise which meant I was home.

We swam a few lengths together, playful, splashing, racing until she was breathless with laughter and I let her win. When she clambered out, I followed, dripping, and we collapsed side by side on the tiles. She leaned against me, wrapped in the towel she'd pulled from a hook, her head resting on my shoulder.

"This place used to mean everything to me," she said softly. "It was where I belonged. But after I failed to qualify for the Olympics, I couldn't bear to come back. I thought I'd lost myself here."

I turned her chin gently, so she met my eyes. "You didn't lose yourself. You found the path that led you to me. To us."

Her lips curved in a small, tremulous smile. "Maybe you're right."

"I am," I murmured, brushing a kiss across her damp hair. "One day, I'll take you to Finfolkaheem. Just like you show me your home now, I will show you mine. My favourite caves, the Archives I used to guard, the clutch-school I went to. But no matter where we go, Elise... You're my home."

She pressed closer, her arm curling around my waist. "And you're mine."

The lights hummed above us, casting the pool in deep shadows. For once, I didn't feel like an outcast or a reject. I was no longer the male deemed unworthy of a mate. I was hers. And that was all I would ever need.

Read on for a little taster of what is to come in Cerban, *the second book in the series!*

Want to know more about Ma'vel and Jonet, the couple whose union was described in the Archives? Read the prequel to the series, Ma'vel, *set in 17th century Scotland, for free!*
skyemackinnon.com/mavel

The Hot Tatties Dating Agency has many clients... meet some hunky alien Highlanders in the Starlight Highlanders *and honourable Norsemen in the* Starlight Vikings*!*

EPILOGUE

Maelis had never been so scared. The beam of her torch sputtered, throwing jagged shadows across the cave walls before shrinking to a weak glow. The battery was almost gone. When it failed, there would be nothing left but darkness.

She shoved again at the boulder that had crashed down from the ceiling. It didn't budge. Her palms stung where stone had pierced her gloves, her muscles trembling with exhaustion. The rock sat wedged in place like a cork in a bottle, sealing her into the underwater cavern.

Her chest ached. Every breath she took drained the last of her dwindling air.

Alone. Trapped. Buried beneath the ocean.

Panic pressed hard at the edges of her mind, but she bit

it back. She shouldn't have come here alone. Foolish. Reckless. Deadly.

They say, at the end, you think of those you love. Maelis didn't. Instead, her thoughts turned unbidden to the strangers who had appeared on the island two weeks ago. The alien mermen with their strange beauty and unreadable eyes.

One of them most of all.

Cerban.

The torch gave a final flicker, then died.

Darkness swallowed her whole.

Continue the story in Cerban*!*

INTERGALACTIC DATING AGENCY

Looking for a love that's out of this world? These strong, smart, sexy aliens are seeking mates from the Milky Way. Just hop onboard with your local Intergalactic Dating Agency! Join a crew of rock star Sci Fi Romance authors as we explore the friendly skies and beyond with trilogies of cosmic craving, astral adventure and otherworldly lovers. Warning: abductions may or may not be included!

Grab more hunky alien action here: romancingthealien.com

THE STARLIGHT UNIVERSE

This book is part of the Starlight Universe, an entire galaxy filled with hunky aliens, exotic planets, and the human women ready to find love among the stars.

Starlight Highlanders Mail Order Brides

Alien Highlanders in kilts come to Earth in search of brides... and take them to planet Albya. Three m/f standalones full of humour, action and steamy romance. Part of the Intergalactic Dating Agency.

Starlight Vikings

Set on Earth and on the spaceship Valkyr, this trilogy of m/f standalones is all about hunky alien Vikings in need of females. Part of the Intergalactic Dating Agency.

Starlight Mermen

Hundreds of years ago, they crash-landed on Earth and gave rise to many of our legends. Now, they're back, desperate for female mates. Part of the Intergalactic Dating Agency.

The Intergalactic Guide to Humans

A humorous take on alien abductions, probing and other shenanigans. One reverse harem trilogy about clueless aliens and the human woman they abducted, followed by several standalone romances with various pairings (m/f, f/m/f and m/m). If you want light entertainment filled with unicorns, fabulous misunderstandings and unusual body parts, this is the series for you.

Starlight Monsters

These aliens are not your usual humanoids... they have claws, fangs, tails, scales, knotty dicks and will growl at you. Interconnected m/f standalones with lots of action, steam and fated mates.

ABOUT THE AUTHOR

Skye MacKinnon is a Scottish romance author who was raised by elves in the mystical Highlands and calls the Loch Ness monster her friend. Her bestselling books weave together romance with action, suspense and whimsical humour, creating page-turners filled with strong heroines, alpha heroes and loveable monsters.

Whether she's writing about aliens in kilts, hunky Vikings or cat shifter assassins, Skye likes to put a new spin on familiar tropes. Some of her heroines don't have to choose, some fall in love with other women, and others get abducted by clueless aliens.

Skye lives with her bossy cat on the west coast of Scotland and uses the dramatic views from her office as an inspiration, no matter whether she writes fantasy, paranormal or science fiction romance. Until she gets abducted by aliens, that is.

Subscribe to her newsletter:
skyemackinnon.com/newsletter

ALSO BY

Find all of Skye's books on her website,
skyemackinnon.com, where you can also order signed
paperbacks and swag.

Many of her books are available as audiobooks.

Science Fiction Romance

Set in the Starlight Universe

- **Starlight Vikings** (sci-fi m/f romance)
- **Starlight Mermen** (sci-fi m/f romance)
- **Starlight Monsters** (sci-fi m/f romance)
- **Starlight Highlanders Mail Order Brides**
  (sci-fi m/f romance)
- **The Intergalactic Guide to Humans** (sci-fi
  romance with various pairings)

Set in other worlds

- **Between Rebels** (sci-fi reverse harem set in the Planet Athion shared world)
- **The Mars Diaries** (sci-fi reverse harem)
- **Aliens and Animals** (f/f sci-fi romance co-written with Arizona Tape)

Paranormal & Fantasy Romance

- **Claiming Her Bears** (post-apocalyptic shifter reverse harem)
- **Daughter of Winter** (fantasy reverse harem)
- **Catnip Assassins** (urban fantasy reverse harem)
- **Infernal Descent** (paranormal reverse harem based on Dante's Inferno, co-written with Bea Paige)
- **Seven Wardens** (fantasy reverse harem co-written with Laura Greenwood)
- **The Lost Siren** (post-apocalyptic, paranormal reverse harem co-written with Liza Street)

Other Series

- **Academy of Time** (time travel academy standalones, reverse harem and m/f)
- **Defiance** (contemporary reverse harem with a hint of thriller/suspense)

Standalones

- Song of Souls – m/f fantasy romance, fairy tale retelling
- Highland Butterflies – sapphic romance
- Wings of Time and Fate - epic fantasy

Box Sets

- Daggers & Destiny – a fantasy romance starter library
- Stars & Seduction - a science fiction romance starter library

Buy your books direct
from the author

GET 20% OFF YOUR NEXT
EBOOK OR AUDIOBOOK!

USE CODE BOOKWORMS AT
SKYEMACKINNON.COM/SHOP

EBOOKS, AUDIOBOOKS, PRINT BOOKS,
MERCHANDISE & MORE

www.ingramcontent.com/pod-product-compliance
Lightning Source LLC
Chambersburg PA
CBHW060555190726
48283CB00003B/1019